# OUTLINE

ALSO BY RACHEL CUSK

FICTION

*The Bradshaw Variations*

*Arlington Park*

*In the Fold*

*The Lucky Ones*

*The Country Life*

*The Temporary*

*Saving Agnes*

NONFICTION

*Aftermath: On Marriage and Separation*

*The Last Supper: A Summer in Italy*

*A Life's Work: On Becoming a Mother*

# OUTLINE

■|■

## Rachel Cusk

■|■

HARPER  PERENNIAL

Published by Harper Perennial, an imprint of HarperCollins Publishers Ltd,
by arrangement with Farrar, Straus and Giroux, LLC.

Originally published in 2014 by Faber and Faber Ltd., Great Britain.
First Published in Canada in 2015 by HarperCollins Publishers Ltd in this
original trade paperback edition.

HarperCollins books may be purchased for educational, business, or sales
promotional use through our Special Markets Department.

HarperCollins Publishers Ltd
2 Bloor Street East, 20th Floor
Toronto, Ontario, Canada
M4W 1A8

*www.harpercollins.ca*

Library and Archives Canada Cataloguing in Publication
information is available upon request

ISBN 978-1-44344-710-2

Printed and bound in the United States of America
RRD 9 8 7 6 5 4 3 2 1

# OUTLINE

# I

Before the flight I was invited for lunch at a London club with a billionaire I'd been promised had liberal credentials. He talked in his open-necked shirt about the new software he was developing, that could help organisations identify the employees most likely to rob and betray them in the future. We were meant to be discussing a literary magazine he was thinking of starting up: unfortunately I had to leave before we arrived at that subject. He insisted on paying for a taxi to the airport, which was useful since I was late and had a heavy suitcase.

The billionaire had been keen to give me the outline of his life story, which had begun unprepossessingly and ended – obviously – with him being the relaxed, well-heeled man who sat across the table from me today. I wondered whether in fact what he wanted now was to be a writer, with the literary magazine as his entrée. A lot of people want to be writers: there was no reason to think you couldn't buy your way into it. This man had bought himself in, and out, of a great many things. He mentioned a scheme he was working on, to eradicate lawyers from people's personal lives. He was also developing a blueprint for a floating wind farm big enough to accommodate the entire community of people needed to service and run it: the gigantic platform could be located far out to sea, thus removing the unsightly turbines from the stretch of coast where he was hoping to pilot the proposal and where, incidentally, he owned a house. On Sundays he played drums in a rock band, just for fun. He was expecting his eleventh child, which wasn't as bad as it sounded when you considered that he and his wife had once adopted quadruplets from Guatemala. I was finding it difficult to assimilate everything I was being told. The waitresses kept bringing more things, oysters, relishes, special wines. He was easily distracted, like a child with too many Christmas presents. But when he put me in the taxi he said, enjoy yourself in Athens, though I didn't remember telling him that was where I was going.

On the tarmac at Heathrow the planeful of people waited silently to be taken into the air. The air hostess stood in the aisle and mimed with her props as the recording played. We were strapped into our seats, a field of strangers, in a silence like the silence of a congregation while the liturgy is read. She showed us the life jacket with its little pipe, the emergency exits, the oxygen mask dangling from a length of clear tubing. She led us through the possibility of death and disaster, as the priest leads the congregation through the details of purgatory and hell; and no one jumped up to escape while there was still time. Instead we listened or half-listened, thinking about other things, as though some special hardness had been bestowed on us by this coupling of formality with doom. When the recorded voice came to the part about the oxygen masks, the hush remained unbroken: no one protested, or spoke up to disagree with this commandment that one should take care of others only after taking care of oneself. Yet I wasn't sure it was altogether true.

On one side of me sat a swarthy boy with lolling knees, whose fat thumbs sped around the screen of a gaming console. On the other was a small man in a pale linen suit, richly tanned, with a silver plume of hair. Outside, the turgid summer afternoon lay stalled over the runway; little airport vehicles raced unconstrained across the flat distances, skating and turning and circling like toys, and further away still was the silver thread of the motorway that ran and glinted like a brook bounded by the monotonous fields. The plane began to move, trundling forward so that the vista appeared to unfreeze into motion, flowing past the windows first slowly and then faster, until there was the feeling of effortful, half-hesitant lifting as it detached itself from the earth. There was a moment in which it seemed impossible that this could happen. But then it did.

The man to my right turned and asked me the reason for my visit to Athens. I said I was going there for work.

'I hope you are staying near water,' he said. 'Athens will be very hot.'

I said I was afraid that was not the case, and he raised his eyebrows, which were silver and grew unexpectedly coarsely and wildly from his forehead, like grasses in a rocky place. It was this eccentricity that had made me answer him. The unexpected sometimes looks like a prompting of fate.

'The heat has come early this year,' he said. 'Normally one is safe until much later. It can be very unpleasant if you aren't used to it.'

In the juddering cabin the lights flickered fitfully on; there was the sound of doors opening and slamming, and tremendous clattering noises, and people were stirring, talking, standing up. A man's voice was talking over the intercom; there was a smell of coffee and food; the air hostesses stalked purposefully up and down the narrow carpeted aisle and their nylon stockings made a rasping sound as they passed. My neighbour told me that he made this journey once or twice a month. He used to keep a flat in London, in Mayfair, 'but these days,' he said with a matter-of-fact set to his mouth, 'I prefer to stay at the Dorchester.'

He spoke a refined and formal kind of English that did not seem wholly natural, as though at some point it had been applied to him carefully with a brush, like paint. I asked him what his nationality was.

'I was sent to an English boarding school at the age of seven,' he replied. 'You might say I have the mannerisms of an Englishman but the heart of a Greek. I am told,' he added, 'it would be much worse the other way around.'

His parents were both Greeks, he continued, but at a certain moment they had relocated the whole household – themselves, four sons, their own parents and an assortment of uncles and aunts – to London, and had begun to conduct themselves in the style of the English upper classes, sending the four boys away to school and establishing a home that became a forum for advantageous social connections, with an inexhaustible stream of aristocrats, politicians and money-makers crossing the threshold. I asked how it was that they had gained access to this foreign milieu, and he shrugged.

'Money is a country all its own,' he said. 'My parents were ship-owners; the family business was an international enterprise, despite the fact that we had lived until now on the small island where both of them were born, an island you would certainly not have heard of, despite its prolixity to some well-known tourist destinations.'

Proximity, I said. I think you mean proximity.

'I do beg your pardon,' he said. 'I mean, of course, proximity.'

But like all wealthy people, he continued, his parents had long outgrown their origins and moved in a borderless sphere among other people of wealth and importance. They retained, of course, a grand house on the island, and that remained their domestic establishment while their children were young; but when the time came to send their sons to school, they relocated themselves to England, where they had many contacts, including some, he said rather proudly, that brought them at least to the peripheries of Buckingham Palace.

Theirs had always been the pre-eminent family of the island: two strains of the local aristocracy had been united by the parental marriage, and what's more, two shipping fortunes consolidated. But the culture of the place was unusual in that it was matriarchal. It was women, not men, who held authority; property was passed not from father to son but from mother to daughter. This, my neighbour said, created familial tensions that were the obverse to those he encountered on his arrival in England. In the world of his childhood, a son was already a disappointment; he himself, the last in a long line of such disappointments, was treated with a special ambivalence, in that his mother wished to believe he was a girl. His hair was kept in long ringlets; he was clothed in dresses and called by the girl's name his parents had chosen in expectation of being given at long last an heir. This unusual situation, my neighbour said, had ancient causes. From its earliest history, the island economy had revolved around the extraction of sponges from the sea bed, and the young men of the community had acquired the skill of deep diving out at sea. But it was a dangerous occupation and hence their life expectancy was extraordinarily low. In this situation, by the repeated death of husbands, the women had gained control of their financial affairs and what's more had passed that control on to their daughters.

'It is hard,' he said, 'to imagine the world as it was in the heyday of my parents, in some ways so pleasurable and in others so callous. For example, my parents had a fifth child, also a boy, whose brain had been damaged at birth, and when the household moved they simply left him there on the island, in the care of a succession of nurses whose credentials – in those days and from that distance – I'm afraid no one cared to investigate too closely.'

He lived there still, an ageing man with the mind of an infant, unable, of course, to give his own side of the story. Meanwhile my neighbour and his brothers entered the chilly waters of an English public school education, learning to think and speak like English boys. My neighbour's ringlets were clipped off, much to his relief, and for the first time in his life he experienced cruelty, and along with it certain new kinds of unhappiness: loneliness, homesickness, the longing for his mother and father. He rifled around in the breast pocket of his suit and took out a soft black leather wallet, from which he extracted a creased monochrome photograph of his parents: a man of rigidly upright bearing in a fitted sort of frock coat buttoned to the throat, whose parted hair and thick straight brows and large scrolled moustache were so black as to give him an appearance of extraordinary ferocity; and beside him, a woman with an unsmiling face as round and hard and inscrutable as a coin. The photograph was taken in the late nineteen-thirties, my neighbour said, before he himself was born. The marriage was already unhappy, however, the father's ferocity and the mother's intransigence being more than cosmetic. Theirs was a tremendous battle of wills, in which no one ever succeeded in separating the combatants; except, very briefly, when they died. But that, he said with a faint smile, is a story for another time.

All this time, the air hostess had been advancing slowly along the aisle, pushing a metal trolley from which she was dispensing plastic trays of food and drink. She had now come to our row: she passed along the white plastic trays, and I offered one to the boy on my left, who silently lifted up his gaming console with both hands so that I could place it on the folded-down table in front of him. My right-hand neighbour and I lifted the lids of ours, so that tea could be poured into the white plastic cups that came with the tray. He began to ask me questions, as though he had learned to remind himself to do so, and I wondered what or who had taught him that lesson, which many people never learn. I said that I lived in London, having very recently moved from the house in the countryside where I had lived alone with my children for the past three years, and where for the seven years before that we had lived together with their father. It had been, in other words, our family home, and I had stayed to watch it become the grave of something I could no longer definitively call either a reality or an illusion.

There was a pause in which we drank our tea, and ate the soft cake-like little biscuits that came with

11

it. Through the windows was a purple near-darkness. The engines roared steadily. The inside of the plane had become darker too, intersected with beams from the overhead spotlights. It was difficult to study my neighbour's face from the adjacent seat but in the light-inflected darkness it had become a landscape of peaks and crevices, from the centre of which rose the extraordinary hook of his nose, casting deep ravines of shadow on either side so that I could barely see his eyes. His lips were thin and his mouth wide and slightly gaping; the part between his nose and upper lip was long and fleshy and he touched it frequently, so that even when he smiled his teeth remained hidden. It was impossible, I said in response to his question, to give the reasons why the marriage had ended: among other things a marriage is a system of belief, a story, and though it manifests itself in things that are real enough, the impulse that drives it is ultimately mysterious. What was real, in the end, was the loss of the house, which had become the geographical location for things that had gone absent and which represented, I supposed, the hope that they might one day return. To move from the house was to declare, in a way, that we had stopped waiting; we could no longer be found at the usual number, the usual address. My younger son, I told him, has the very annoying habit of immediately leaving the place where you have agreed to meet him, if you aren't there when he arrives. Instead he goes in search of you, and becomes frustrated and lost. I couldn't find you! he cries afterwards, invariably aggrieved. But the only hope of finding anything is to stay exactly where you are, at the agreed place. It's just a question of how long you can hold out.

'My first marriage,' my neighbour replied, after a pause, 'often seems to me to have ended for the silliest of reasons. When I was a boy I used to watch the hay-carts coming back from the fields, so overloaded it seemed a miracle they didn't tip. They would jolt up and down and sway alarmingly from side to side, but amazingly they never went over. And then one day I saw it, the cart on its side, the hay spilled all over the place, people running around shouting. I asked what had happened and the man told me they had hit a bump in the road. I always remembered that,' he said, 'how inevitable it seemed and yet how silly. And it was the same with my first wife and me,' he said. 'We hit a bump in the road, and over we went.'

It had, he now realised, been a happy relationship, the most harmonious of his life. He and his wife had met and got engaged as teenagers; they had never argued, until the argument in which everything between them was broken. They had two children, and had amassed considerable wealth: they had a large house outside Athens, a London flat, a place in Geneva; they had horses and skiing holidays and a forty-foot yacht moored in the waters of the Aegean. They were both still young enough to believe that this principle of growth was exponential; that life was only expansive, and broke the successive vessels in which you tried to contain it in its need to expand more. After the argument, reluctant to move definitively out of the house, my neighbour went to live on the yacht in its mooring. It was summer and the yacht was luxurious; he could swim, and fish, and entertain friends. For a few weeks he lived in a state of pure illusion which was really numbness, like the numbness that follows an injury, before pain starts to make its way through it, slowly but relentlessly finding a path through the dense analgesic fog. The weather broke; the yacht became cold and uncomfortable. His wife's father summoned him to a meeting at which he was asked to relinquish any claim on their shared assets, and he agreed. He believed he could afford to be generous, that he would make it all back again. He was thirty-six years old and still felt the force of exponential growth in his veins, of life straining to burst the vessel in which it had been contained. He could have it all again, with the difference that this time he would want what he had.

'Though I have discovered,' he said, touching his fleshy upper lip, 'that that is harder than it sounds.'

All this did not, of course, come to pass as he had imagined it. The bump in the road hadn't only up-set his marriage; it caused him to veer off on to a different road altogether, a road that was but a long, directionless detour, a road he had no real business being on and that sometimes he still felt himself to be travelling even to this day. Like the loose stitch that causes the whole garment to unravel, it was hard to piece back this chain of events to its original flaw. Yet these events had constituted the majority of his adult life. It was nearly thirty years since his first marriage ended, and the further he got from that life, the more real it became to him. Or not real exactly, he said – what had happened since had been real enough. The word he was looking for was authentic: his first mar-riage had been authentic in a way that nothing ever had again. The older he got, the more it represented to him a kind of home, a place to which he yearned to return. Though when he remembered it honestly, and even more so when he actually spoke to his first wife – which these days was rarely – the old feelings of constriction would return. All the same, it seemed to him now that that life had been lived almost un-consciously, that he had been lost in it, absorbed in it, as you can be absorbed in a book, believing in its events and living entirely through and with its characters. Never again since had he been able to absorb himself; never again had he been able to believe in that way. Perhaps it was that – the loss of belief – that constituted his yearning for the old life. Whatever it was, he and his wife had built things that had flourished, had together expanded the sum of what they were and what they had; life had responded willingly to them, had treated them abundantly, and this – he now saw – was what had given him the confidence to break it all, break it with what now seemed to him to be an extraordinary casualness, because he thought there would be more.

More what? I asked.

'More – life,' he said, opening his hands in a gesture of receipt. 'And more affection,' he added, after a pause. 'I wanted more affection.'

He replaced the photograph of his parents in his wallet. There was now blackness at the windows. In the cabin people were reading, sleeping, talking. A man in long baggy shorts walked up and down the aisle jiggling a baby on his shoulder. The plane seemed stilled, almost motionless; there was so little interface between inside and outside, so little friction, that it was hard to believe we were moving forward. The electric light, with the absolute darkness outside, made people look very fleshly and real, their detail

16

so unmediated, so impersonal, so infinite. Each time the man with the baby passed I saw the network of creases in his shorts, his freckled arms covered in coarse reddish fur, the pale, mounded skin of his midriff where his T-shirt had ridden up, and the tender wrinkled feet of the baby on his shoulder, the little hunched back, the soft head with its primitive whorl of hair.

My neighbour turned to me again, and asked me what work it was that was taking me to Athens. For the second time I felt the conscious effort of his enquiry, as though he had trained himself in the recovery of objects that were falling from his grasp. I remembered the way, when each of my sons was a baby, they would deliberately drop things from their high chair in order to watch them fall to the floor, an activity as delightful to them as its consequences were appalling. They would stare down at the fallen thing – a half-eaten rusk, or a plastic ball – and become increasingly agitated by its failure to return. Eventually they would begin to cry, and usually found that the fallen object came back to them by that route. It always surprised me that their response to this chain of events was to repeat it: as soon as the object was in their hands they would drop it again, leaning over to watch it fall. Their delight never lessened, and nor did their distress. I always expected that at some point they would realise the distress was unnecessary and would choose to avoid it, but they never did. The memory of suffering had no effect whatever on what they elected to do: on the contrary, it compelled them to repeat it, for the suffering was the magic that caused the object to come back and allowed the delight in dropping it to become possible again. Had I refused to return it the very first time they dropped it, I suppose they would have learned something very different, though what that might have been I wasn't sure.

I told him I was a writer, and was going to Athens for a couple of days to teach a course at a summer school there. The course was entitled 'How to Write': a number of different writers were teaching on it, and since there is no one way to write I supposed we would give the students contradictory advice. They were mostly Greeks, I had been told, though for the purposes of this course they were expected to write in English. Other people were sceptical about that idea but I didn't see what was wrong with it. They could write in whatever language they wanted: it made no difference to me. Sometimes, I said, the loss of transition became the gain of simplicity. Teaching was just a way of making a living, I continued. But I had one or two friends in Athens I might see while I was there.

A writer, my neighbour said, inclining his head in a gesture that could have conveyed either respect for the profession or a total ignorance of it. I had noticed, when I first sat down beside him, that he was reading a well-thumbed Wilbur Smith: this, he now said, was not entirely representative of his reading tastes, though it was true he lacked discrimination where fiction was concerned. His interest was in books of information, of facts and the interpretation of facts, and he was confident that he was not unsophisticated here in his preferences. He could recognise a fine prose style; one of his favourite writers, for example, was John Julius Norwich. But in fiction, admittedly, he was uneducated. He removed the Wilbur Smith from the seat pocket, where it still remained, and plunged it into the briefcase at his feet so that it was out of sight, as though wishing to disown it, or perhaps thinking that I might forget I had seen it. As it happened I was no longer interested in literature as a form of snobbery or even of self-definition – I had no desire to prove that one book was better than another: in fact, if I read something I admired I found myself increasingly disinclined to mention it at all. What I knew personally to be true had come to seem unrelated to the process of persuading others. I did not, any longer, want to persuade anyone of anything.

19

'My second wife,' my neighbour said presently, 'had never read a book in her life.'

She was absolutely ignorant, he continued, even of basic history and geography, and would say the most embarrassing things in company without any sense of shame at all. On the contrary, it angered her when people spoke of things she had no knowledge of: when a Venezuelan friend came to visit, for instance, she refused to believe that such a country existed because she had never heard of it. She herself was English, and so exquisitely beautiful it was hard not to credit her with some inner refinement; but though her nature did contain some surprises, they were not of a particularly pleasant kind. He often invited her parents to stay, as though by studying them he might decipher the mystery of their daughter. They would come to the island, where the ancestral home still remained, and would stay for weeks at a time. Never had he met people of such extraordinary blandness, such featurelessness: however much he exhausted himself with trying to stimulate them, they were as unresponsive as a pair of armchairs. In the end he became very fond of them, as one can become fond of armchairs; particularly the father, whose boundless reticence was so extreme that gradually my neighbour came to understand that he must suffer from some form of psychic injury. It moved him to see someone so injured by life. In his younger days he almost certainly wouldn't even have noticed the man, let alone pondered the causes of his silence; and in this way, in recognising his father-in-law's suffering, he began to recognise his own. It sounds trivial, yet it could almost be said that through this recognition he felt his whole life turning on its axis: the history of his self-will appeared to him, by a simple revolution in perspective, as a moral journey. He had turned around, like a climber turns around and looks back down the mountain, reviewing the path he has travelled, no longer immersed in the ascent.

A long time ago – so long that he had forgotten the author's name – he read some memorable lines in a story about a man who is trying to translate another story, by a much more famous author. In these lines – which, my neighbour said, he still remembers to this day – the translator says that a sentence is born into this world neither good nor bad, and that to establish its character is a question of the subtlest possible adjustments, a process of intuition to which exaggeration and force are fatal. Those lines concerned the art of writing, but looking around himself in early middle age my neighbour began to see that they applied just as much to the art of living. Everywhere he looked he saw people as it were ruined by the extremity of their own experiences, and his new

21

parents-in-law appeared to be a case in point. What was clear, in any case, was that their daughter had mistaken him for a far wealthier man: the fatal yacht, on which he had hidden out as a marital escapee and which was his sole remaining asset from that time, had lured her. She had a great need for luxury and he began to work as he never had before, blindly and frantically, spending all his time in meetings and on airplanes, negotiating and securing deals, taking on more and more risk in order to provide her with the wealth she took for granted was there. He was, in effect, manufacturing an illusion: no matter what he did, the gap between illusion and reality could never be closed. Gradually, he said, this gap, this distance between how things were and how I wanted them to be, began to undermine me. I felt myself becoming empty, he said, as though I had been living until now on the reserves I had accumulated over the years and they had gradually dwindled away.

It was now that the propriety of his first wife, the health and prosperity of their family life and the depth of their shared past, began to smite him. The first wife, after a period of unhappiness, had married again: she had become, after their divorce, quite fixated on skiing, going to northern Europe and the mountains whenever she could, and before long had declared herself married to an instructor in Lech who had given

her back, so she said, her confidence. That m
my neighbour admitted, remained intact to
But back in the time of its inception, my r
had begun to realise he had made a mistake,
endeavoured to restore contact with his first wife, with
what intentions he wasn't quite clear. Their two children, a boy and a girl, were still quite small: it was
reasonable enough, after all, that they should be in
touch. Dimly he remembered that in the period immediately following their separation, it was she who was
always trying to get hold of him; and remembered too
that he had avoided her calls, intent as he was on the
pursuit of the woman who was now his second wife.
He was unavailable, gone into a new world in which
his first wife appeared barely to exist, in which she was
a kind of ridiculous cardboard figure whose actions –
so he persuaded himself and others – were the actions
of a madwoman. But now it was she who could not be
found: she was plunging down cold white mountainsides in the Arlberg, where he did not exist for her any
more than she had existed for him. She didn't answer
his calls, or answered them curtly, distractedly, saying
she had to go. She could not be called upon to recognise him, and this was the most bewildering thing of
all, for it made him feel absolutely unreal. It was with
her, after all, that his identity had been forged: if she
no longer recognised him, then who was he?

23

The strange thing is, he said, that even now, when these events are long in the past and he and his first wife communicate more regularly, she only has to speak for more than a minute and she begins to irritate him. And he didn't doubt that had she rushed back from the mountains, in the time when he seemed to have had a change of heart, she would quickly have come to irritate him so much that the whole demise of their relationship would have been re-enacted. Instead they have grown older at a distance: when he speaks to her he imagines quite clearly the life they would have had, the life they would be sharing now. It is like walking past a house you used to live in: the fact that it still exists, so concrete, makes everything that has happened since seem somehow insubstantial. Without structure, events are unreal: the reality of his wife, like the reality of the house, was structural, determinative. It had limitations, which he encounters when he hears his wife on the telephone. Yet the life without limitations has been exhausting, has been one long history of actual and emotional expense, like thirty years of living in one hotel after another. It is the feeling of impermanence, of homelessness, that has cost him. He has spent and spent to rid himself of that feeling, to put a roof over his own head. And all the time he sees at a distance his home – his wife – standing there, essentially unchanged, but belonging to other people now.

I said that the way he had told his story rather proved that point, because I couldn't see the second wife half as clearly as I could see the first. In fact, I didn't entirely believe in her. She was rolled out as an all-purpose villain, but what wrong, really, had she done? She had never pretended to be an intellectual, as for instance my neighbour had pretended to be rich, and since she had been valued entirely for her beauty, it was natural – some would say sensible – that she should want to put a price on it. And as for Venezuela, who was he to say what someone ought or ought not to know? There was plenty, I felt sure, that he himself didn't know, and what he didn't know didn't exist for him, any more than Venezuela existed for his pretty wife. My neighbour frowned so deeply that clownish furrows appeared on either side of his chin.

'I admit,' he said after a long pause, 'that on this subject I may be somewhat biased.'

The truth was that he could not forgive his second wife her treatment of his children, who spent the school holidays with them, usually at the old family house on the island. She was particularly jealous of the eldest, a boy, whose every movement she criticised. She watched him with an obsessiveness that was quite extraordinary to behold, and she was always putting him to work around the house, blaming him for the smallest evidence of disorder and insisting on her right to punish him for what she alone thought of as misdemeanours. Once, he returned to the house to find that the boy had been shut in the extensive, catacomb-like cellars that ran all the way under the building, a dark and sinister place at the best of times, where he himself used to be afraid to go as a child. He was lying on his side, shaking, and told his father he had been put there for failing to clear his plate from the table. It was as though he represented everything that was burdensome in her wifely role, as though he were the incarnation of some injustice she felt pinioned by: and he was the proof, too, that she had not come first and never would, so far as her husband was concerned.

He could never understand this need of hers for primacy, for after all it wasn't his fault that he had lived a life before he met her; but increasingly she seemed bent on the destruction of that history, and of the children who were its ineradicable evidence. They had, by then, a child of their own, also a boy, but far from rounding things out this had only seemed to make her jealousy worse. She accused him of not loving their son as much as he loved his older children; she watched him constantly for evidence of favour, and in fact she favoured their own child blatantly, but she was often angry with the little boy too, as though she felt that a different child could have won this battle for her. And indeed she more or less abandoned their son, when the end came. They were spending the summer on the island, and her parents – the armchairs – were there too. He was fonder of them than ever by now, for he saw their flatness, sympathetically, as the evidence of their daughter's cyclonic nature. They were like a terrain forever being hit by tornadoes; they lived in a state of permanent semi-devastation. His wife got it into her head that she wanted to return to Athens: she was bored, he supposed, on the island; there were probably parties she wanted to go to, things she wanted to do; she had got tired of always spending the summers here, in the family mausoleum; and besides, her parents were due to fly back shortly from Athens, so they could all go together, she said, leaving the older children here in the care of the housekeeper. My neighbour replied that he couldn't go to Athens now. He couldn't possibly leave his children – they were staying with him for another two or three weeks. How could he desert them, when this was the only time he had with them? Well if he didn't come, she said, he could quite simply consider their marriage to be over.

This was, then, the actual contest: finally he was being asked to choose, and of course it felt to him like no choice at all. It felt utterly unreasonable, and a terrible argument ensued, at the end of which his wife, their son and her parents boarded a boat and returned to Athens. Before they left, his father-in-law made a rare excursion into speech. What he said was that he could see it from my neighbour's point of view. It was the last my neighbour ever saw of them, and more or less the last he ever saw of his wife, who returned with her parents to England and from there divorced him. She hired a very good lawyer, and he found himself near financial ruin for the second time in his life. He sold the yacht, and bought a small motor boat that reflected the state of his fortunes more accurately. Their son, though, came drifting back once his mother remarried, having found herself an English aristocrat of demonstrably enormous wealth – and discovered that the child impeded her second marriage in much the same way my neighbour's children had impeded his. In this last detail there was evidence if not of his ex-wife's integrity, then at least of a certain consistency.

So much is lost, he said, in the shipwreck. What remains are fragments, and if you don't hold on to them the sea will take them too. Yet I still, he said, believe in love. Love restores almost everything, and where it can't restore, it takes away the pain. For example, you, he said to me – at the moment you're sad, but if you were in love the sadness would stop. Sitting there I thought again of my sons in their high chairs, and of their discovery that distress magically made the ball come back. At that moment the plane took its first, gentle lurch downward in the darkness. A voice began to speak over the intercom; the air hostesses began to stalk up and down, herding people back into their seats. My neighbour asked me for my telephone number: perhaps we could have dinner some time, while I was in Athens.

I remained dissatisfied by the story of his second marriage. It had lacked objectivity; it relied too heavily on extremes, and the moral properties it ascribed to those extremes were often incorrect. It was not wrong, for instance, to be jealous of a child, though it was certainly very painful for all concerned. I found I did not believe certain key facts, for instance that his wife had locked his son in the cellar, and nor was I entirely convinced by her beauty, which again seemed to me to have been misappropriated. If it wasn't wrong to be jealous, it certainly wasn't wrong to be beautiful: the wrong lay in the beauty being stolen, as it were, by the narrator, under false pretences. Reality might be described as the eternal

29

equipoise of positive and negative, but in this story the two poles had become dissociated and ascribed separate, warring identities. The narrative invariably showed certain people – the narrator and his children – in a good light, while the wife was brought in only when it was required of her to damn herself further. The narrator's treacherous attempts to contact his first wife, for instance, were given a positive, empathetic status, while his second wife's insecurity – well founded, as we now knew – was treated as an incomprehensible crime. The one exception was the narrator's love for his boring, tornado-swept parents-in-law, a bittersweet detail in which positive and negative regained their balance. But otherwise this was a story in which I sensed the truth was being sacrificed to the narrator's desire to win.

My neighbour laughed, and said that I was probably right. My parents fought all their lives, he said, and no one ever won. But no one ran away either. It is the children who have run away. My brother has been married five times, he said, and on Christmas Day he sits alone in his apartment in Zurich, counting his money and eating a cheese sandwich. Tell me the truth, I said: did she really lock your son in the cellar? He inclined his head.

'She always denied it,' he said. 'She claimed Takis had shut himself in there, to get her into trouble.'

But I do accept, he said, that it was not unreasonable for her to want me to go to Athens. He hadn't quite given me the full story – in fact her mother had been taken ill. It was nothing too serious, but she needed to be admitted to the hospital on the mainland, and his wife's Greek wasn't all that good. But he thought they could manage, his wife and her father together. The father-in-law's parting remark, then, was more ambivalent than, in the first version, it had seemed. We had by now fastened our seat-belts, as the voice on the intercom had asked us to, and for the first time I saw lights below as we swung quivering downwards, a great forest of lights rising and falling mysteriously through the darkness.

In those days I was so worried all the time about my children, my neighbour said. I couldn't think about what I needed or what she needed; I thought they needed me more. His words reminded me of the oxygen masks, which had not, of course, put in an appearance over the past few hours. It was a kind of mutual cynicism, I said, that had resulted in the oxygen masks being provided, on the tacit understanding that they would never be needed. My neighbour said he had found that to be true of many aspects of life, but that all the same the law of averages was not something it paid to base your personal expectations on.

## II

I noticed that when we walked along narrow stretches of pavement beside the roaring traffic, Ryan always took the place on the inside.

'I've been reading up on statistics for road deaths in Athens,' he said. 'I'm taking this information very seriously. I owe it to my family to get home in one piece.'

There were often dogs lying collapsed across the pavement, big ones with extravagant shaggy pelts. They were insensate in the heat, motionless except for the breath faintly moving in their sides. From a distance they sometimes looked like women in fur coats who had fallen down drunk.

'Do you step over a dog?' Ryan said, hesitating. 'Or do you walk around it?'

He didn't mind the heat, he said – in fact he was enjoying it. He felt like years of damp were drying out. His only regret was that it had taken him till the age of forty-one to get here, because it seemed like a really fascinating place. It was a shame the wife and kids couldn't see it too, but he was determined not to ruin it by feeling guilty. The wife had had a weekend with her girlfriends in Paris just now, leaving him to take care of the kids alone; there was no reason he shouldn't feel he'd earned it. And to be perfectly honest, the kids slowed you down: first thing this morning he'd walked up to the Acropolis, before the heat got too intense, and he couldn't have done that with them in tow, could he? And even if he had, he'd have spent the whole time worrying about sunburn and dehydration, and though he might have seen the Parthenon sitting like a gold and white crumbling crown on the hilltop with the fierce pagan blue of the sky behind, he wouldn't have felt it, as he was able to feel it this morning, airing the shaded crevices of his being. Walking up there, for some reason he'd remembered how, in the bedroom of his childhood, the sheets always smelled of mould. If you opened a cupboard in his parents' house, as often as not there'd be water running down the back of it. When he left Tralee for Dublin, he found that all his books were stuck to the shelves when he tried to take them down. Beckett and Synge had rotted and turned to glue.

'Which suggests I wasn't much of a reader,' he said, 'so it's not a detail I give out that often.'

No, he had never been to Greece before, nor to any country where you could take the sun for granted.

His wife was allergic to it in any case – to the sun, that was. Like him she'd been raised in the damp and shade and the sun brought her out in purple spots and blisters; she couldn't cope with heat at all, which induced migraines and vomiting. They took the kids to Galway for holidays, where her parents had a house, and if they were desperate for a break from Dublin they could always go back to Tralee. It's a case of home is where when you have to go there they have to take you in, he said. And his wife believed in all that, in the family network and Sunday lunch and children having grandparents on both sides, but if it was left to him he'd probably never cross his parents' threshold again. Not that they did anything particularly wrong, he said, they're nice enough people, I just don't think it would occur to me.

We passed a café with tables in the shade of a large awning, and the people sitting at the tables looked superior, so cool and watchful in the shadows while we toiled incomprehensibly through the heat and turmoil of the street. Ryan said he might stop and drink something; he'd come here earlier, he said, for breakfast, and it had seemed like a nice place. It wasn't clear whether he wanted me to sit down with him or not. In fact he had phrased it so carefully that I got the impression inclusion was something he actually avoided. After that I observed him for this

34

characteristic, and I noticed that when other people were making plans, Ryan would always say 'I might come along later' or 'I might see you there' rather than commit himself to a time and place. He would only tell you what he was doing after he'd done it. I met him by chance once in the street and noticed that his slicked-back hair was wet, so I had asked him outright where he'd been. He admitted he'd just swum at the Hilton hotel, which had a large outdoor pool, where he had posed as a guest and done forty lengths along-side Russian plutocrats and American businessmen and girls with surgically enhanced bodies. He had felt sure the pool attendants were watching him, but no one had dared interrogate him. How else were you meant to exercise, he wanted to know, in the middle of a traffic-choked city in forty degrees of heat?

At the table he sat, like the other men, with his back to the wall so that his view was of the café and the street. I sat opposite him, and because he was all I could see I looked at him. Ryan was teaching alongside me at the summer school: from a distance he was a man of conventional sandy-coloured good looks, but close up there was something uneasy in his appearance, as though he had been put together out of unrelated elements, so that the different parts of him didn't entirely go together. He had large white teeth which he kept always a little bared and a loose body poised somewhere between muscle and fat, but his head was small and narrow, with sparse, almost colourless hair that grew in spikes back from his forehead and colourless eyelashes that were hidden for now behind dark glasses. His eyebrows, however, were fierce and straight and black. When the waitress came he took the glasses off and I saw his eyes, two small bright blue chips in slightly reddened whites. The rims were red too, as though they were sore, or as though the sun had singed them. He asked the waitress if she had non-alcoholic beer and she leaned towards him with her hand cupped around her ear, not understanding. He picked up the menu and together they studied it.

'Are any of these beers,' he said slowly, running a tutelary finger down the list and glancing at her frequently, 'non-alcoholic?'

She leaned closer, scrutinising the place where his finger pointed, while his eyes fixed themselves on her face, which was young and beautiful, with long ringlets of hair on either side which she kept tucking behind her ears. Because he was pointing at something that wasn't there her bewilderment was long-lasting, and in the end she said she would have to go and get her manager, at which point he closed the menu like a teacher finishing a lesson and said not to worry, he would just have an ordinary beer

36

after all. This change of plan confused her further: the menu was opened again and the whole lesson repeated, and I found my attention straying to the people at other tables and out to the street, where cars passed and dogs lay in heaps of fur in the glare.

'She served me this morning,' Ryan said when the waitress had gone. 'The same girl. They're beautiful people, aren't they? It's a shame she didn't have the beer, though. You can get that everywhere at home.'

He said that he was seriously trying to cut down his drinking; the past year he'd basically been on a health kick, going to the gym every day and eating salad. He'd let things slide a bit when the kids were born, and anyway it was hard to be healthy in Ireland; the whole culture of the place militated against it. In his youth in Tralee he was pretty seriously overweight, like a lot of the people there, including his parents and his older brother, who still regarded chips as one of their five a day. He'd had a number of allergies too, eczema and asthma, which no doubt weren't helped by the family diet. As a child at school they'd had to wear shorts with knee-high woollen socks, and the socks would adhere horribly to his eczema. He still remembered peeling them off at bedtime and half the skin of his legs coming off with them. These days, of course, you'd rush your child off to a dermatologist or a homeopath, but then you were just left to get on with it. When he had breathing difficulties, his parents would put him out to sit in the car. As for the weight, he said, you rarely saw yourself with your clothes off, or anyone else without theirs for that matter. He remembered the feeling of estrangement from his own body, as it laboured in the damp, spore-ridden climate of the house; his clogged lungs and itchy skin, his veins full of sugar and fat, his wobbling flesh shrouded in uncomfortable clothing. As a teenager he was self-conscious and sedentary and avoided any physical exposure of himself. But then he spent a year in America, on a writing programme there, and had discovered that by effort of will he could make himself look completely different. There was a pool and a gym on campus, and food he had never even heard of – sprouts and wholegrains and soya – in the cafeteria; and not only that, he was surrounded by people for whom the notion of self-transformation was an article of faith. He picked it up almost overnight, the whole concept: he could decide how he wanted to be and then be it. There was no pre-ordination; that sense of the self as a destiny and a doom that had hung like a pall over his whole life could stay, he now realised, behind him in Ireland. On his first visit to the gym he saw a beautiful girl exercising on a machine while at the same time reading from a large book of philosophy that lay open on a stand in front of her, and he could hardly believe his own eyes. He discovered that all the machines in that gym had bookstands. This machine was called a step machine, and it simulated the action of walking upstairs: from then on he always used it, and always with a book open in front of him, for the image of that girl – who to his not inconsiderable disappointment he never saw again – had fixed itself in his head. Over the course of the year he must have ascended miles' worth of stairs while remaining in one place, and that was the image he had internalised, not just of the girl but of the imaginary staircase itself, and of himself forever climbing it with a book dangled just in front of him like a carrot in front of a donkey. Climbing that staircase was the work he had to do to separate himself from the place from which he had come.

It was more than just a stroke of luck, he said, that he happened to go to America: it was the defining episode of his life, and when he thought about what he would have been and what he would have done had that episode not occurred it frightened him in a way. It was his English tutor at college who told him about the writing programme and encouraged him to apply. By the time the letter came college was over and he was back in Tralee, living in his parents' house and working at a chicken-processing plant, and having an affair with a woman much older

39

than himself who had two kids he didn't doubt she'd got him lined up to play father to. The letter said that he'd been offered a scholarship, on the basis of the writing sample he'd submitted, with a paid second year to follow if he wanted to earn himself a teaching qualification. Forty-eight hours later he was gone, taking a few books and the clothes he stood up in, on an airplane and leaving the British Isles for the first time in his life, and without a clue really where he was going, except that sitting above the clouds it appeared to be heaven.

In fact it so happened, he said, that his older brother left for America at more or less the same time. He and his brother never had all that much to say to each other, and at the time he was barely aware of Kevin's plans, but thinking about it now it was quite a coincidence, except that Kevin hadn't had a stroke of luck to send him on his way. Instead he'd joined the US Marines, and probably at much the same time as Ryan was treading the step machine, Kevin was also shedding the flab of Tralee at boot camp. For all Ryan knew he might have been down the road, though America is a big place and it was unlikely. And of course the job involves a lot of travel, Ryan said, with apparent sincerity. By a further coincidence both brothers returned to Ireland three years later and met in their parents' sitting room, both of them now fit and lean; Ryan with a teaching qualification, a book contract and a ballet-dancer girlfriend, and Kevin with a grotesquely tattooed body and a mental condition that meant his life would never again be his own. The imaginary staircase went down, it seemed, as well as up: Ryan and his brother were now effectively members of two different social classes, and while Ryan went off to Dublin to take up a university teaching post, Kevin returned to the damp bedroom of their childhood, where excepting the odd stay in mental institutions, he has remained ever since. The funny thing is, Ryan said, that their parents took no more pride in Ryan's achievements than they accepted blame for Kevin's collapse. They tried to get rid of Kevin and have him committed on a permanent basis, but he kept being sent back to them, the perennial bad penny. And yet they were also faintly scornful of Ryan, the writer and university lecturer, living now in a nice house in Dublin and about to marry, not the ballet dancer but an Irish girl, a college friend from the time before America. What Ryan had learned from this is that your failures keep returning to you, while your successes are something you always have to convince yourself of.

His narrow blue eyes fixed themselves on the young waitress, who was approaching through the shade with our drinks.

'Oh, run away with me,' he said, as she leaned over him to place his glass on the table. I thought she must have heard him, but he had judged it precisely: her superb, statue-like countenance didn't flicker. 'What people,' he said, still watching her while she walked away. He asked whether I was at all familiar with the country and I said that I had come here, to Athens, on a somewhat fateful holiday with my children three years earlier.

'They're beautiful people,' he replied. After a while he said that he supposed it wasn't all that hard to explain, when you considered the climate and the way of life, and of course the diet here. When you looked at the Irish you saw centuries of rain and rotten potatoes. He still had to fight it in himself, that feeling of contaminated flesh; it was so hard to feel clean in Ireland, the way he'd felt in America, or the way you felt here. I asked him why he had come back, after he finished his Masters, and he said there were a lot of reasons, though no one of them was particularly powerful. It was just that all together they amounted to enough to nudge him back. One of them, in fact, was the very thing he had liked most about America at first, which was the feeling that no one really came from anywhere. I mean obviously, he said, they had to have come from somewhere, but there wasn't the same feeling of your home town waiting to claim

you, that sense of pre-ordination that he had miracu-
lously felt himself climbing clear of as he first rose
above the clouds. His fellow students made much of
his Irishness, he said: he found himself playing up to
it, putting on the accent and all that, until he'd almost
convinced himself that being Irish was an identity in
itself. And after all, what other identity did he have?
It frightened him a little, the idea of not coming from
somewhere; he began to see himself as not cursed
but blessed, began almost to rekindle that sense of
pre-ordination, or at least to see it in a different light.
And writing, the whole concept of transmuted pain
– Ireland was the structure for that, his own past in
Tralee was the structure for that. He suddenly felt he
might not cope with the fundamental anonymity of
America. To be perfectly honest, he wasn't the most
talented student on that programme – he had no problem admitting that – and one reason, he'd decided,
was this same anonymity his peers had to grapple
with and he didn't. It made you a better writer, did it
not, not having an identity to fall back on: you saw
the world with less troubled eyes. And he was more
Irish in America than he'd ever been at home.

He began to see Dublin as he used to see it in his
mind's eye as a schoolboy, with scholars on bicycles
sailing like dark swans through the streets in their
black robes. Might what he had seen all those years

before be himself? A dark swan, gliding through the protected city, free within its walls; not the American version of freedom, big and flat and borderless as a prairie. He came back in a moderate blaze of glory, with his teaching job and his ballet dancer and his book contract. The ballet dancer went home six months later, and the book – a book of short stories, well received – remains his only published work. He and Nancy are still in touch: in fact, they talked on Facebook only the other day. She doesn't dance any more – she's become a psychotherapist, though to be honest she's a little bit crazy herself. She lives with her mother in an apartment in New York City, and even though she's forty years old it strikes Ryan that she is unchanged, that she is more or less exactly the same as she was at twenty-three. And there's him with his wife and his kids and his house in Dublin, a different man in every way. Stunted, is what he sometimes thinks about her, though he knows it's unkind. She's always asking him if he's written another book yet, and in a way he'd like to ask her in return – though of course he never would – whether she's had a life yet.

As for the stories, he still likes them, still picks them up and reads them now and then. They get reproduced every so often in anthologies; a little while ago his agent sold the rights to a publishing house in

Albania. But in a way it's like looking at old photographs of yourself. There comes a point at which the record needs to be updated, because you've shed too many links with what you were. He doesn't quite know how it happened; all he knows is that he doesn't recognise himself in those stories any more, though he remembers the bursting feeling of writing them, something in himself massing and pushing irresistibly to be born. He hasn't had that feeling since; he almost thinks that to remain a writer he'd have to become one all over again, when he might just as easily become an astronaut, or a farmer. It's as if he can't quite remember what drove him into words in the first place, all those years before, yet words are what he still deals in. I suppose it's a bit like marriage, he said. You build a whole structure on a period of intensity that's never repeated. It's the basis of your faith and sometimes you doubt it, but you never renounce it because too much of your life stands on that ground. Though the temptation can be extreme, he added, as the young waitress glided past our table. I must have looked disapproving, because he said:

'My wife eyeballs the fellas, when she's out for the night with her friends. I'd be disappointed if she didn't. Take a good look, is what I say. See what's out there. And she's just the same – go on, feel free to look.'

45

I remembered then an evening I'd spent in a bar a few years ago, with a group of people that included a married couple I didn't know. The woman kept identifying attractive girls and drawing her husband's attention to them; they sat there and discussed the attributes of the various girls, and were it not for the grimace of utter desperation I glimpsed on the woman's face when she thought no one was looking, I would have believed this was an activity both of them enjoyed.

He and his wife had a good partnership, Ryan said. They shared the work of the kids and the house – his wife was no martyr, as his mother had been. She went off on her own holidays with her girlfriends and expected him to take care of everything in her absence: when they gave one another freedoms, it was on the understanding that they would claim those same freedoms themselves. If it sounds a little bit calculated, Ryan said, that doesn't worry me at all. There's a business aspect to running a household. It's best if everyone's honest right at the start about what they're going to need, to be able to stay in it.

My phone sounded on the table in front of me. It was a text from my son: *Where's my tennis racket?* I don't know about you, Ryan said, but I actually don't have the time to write, what with the family and the teaching job. Especially the teaching – it's the teaching that sucks the life out of you. And when I do have a week to myself, I spend it teaching extra courses like this one, for the money. If it's a choice between paying the mortgage and writing a story that'll only see the light of day in some tiny literary magazine – I know that for some people there's a need, or so they say, but for a lot of them I think it's more that they like the life, they like saying that's what they are, a writer. I'm not saying I don't like it myself, but it isn't the be-all and end-all. I'd just as soon write a thriller, to be perfectly honest. Go where the real money is – one or two of my own students, he said, have taken that road, you know, written things that have gone global in some cases. Actually it was the wife who said it – wasn't it you taught them how to do that? Obviously she doesn't entirely understand the process, but in a way she's got a point. And if there's one thing I know it's that writing comes out of tension, tension between what's inside and what's outside. Surface tension, isn't that the phrase – actually that's not a bad title, is it? He sat back in his chair and stared meditatively towards the street. I wondered whether he had already decided on *Surface Tension* as the title for his thriller. In any case, he continued, when I think back to the conditions that made me write *The Homecoming*, I realise there's no point me trying to get back to that place because I never could. I could never reproduce that particular tension in myself: life is sending you in one direction and you're pulling away in another, like you're disagreeing with your own destiny, like who you are is in disagreement with who they say you are. Your whole soul is in revolt, he said. He drained his glass of beer in one swallow. What am I in revolt against now? Three kids and a mortgage and a job I'd like to see a bit less of, that's what.

My phone sounded again. It was a text from my neighbour on last night's plane. He was thinking of taking his boat out, he said, and wondered whether I'd like to join him for a swim. He could come and collect me at my apartment in an hour or so, and drive me back there afterwards. I thought about it while Ryan was talking. What I miss, Ryan said, is the discipline itself. In a way I don't care what I write – I just want that feeling of being in sync again, body and mind, do you know what I mean? As he spoke I saw the imaginary staircase rising in front of him once more, stretching out of sight; and him climbing it, with a book suspended tantalisingly ahead of him. The perimeter of shade had receded and the glare of the street advanced, so that we now sat almost at the interface of the two. The commotion of heat was just at my back; I edged my chair in towards the table. When you're in that place you make time for it, don't you, Ryan said, the way people make time to have affairs. I mean, you never hear someone say they wanted to have an affair but they couldn't find the time, do you? No matter how busy you are, no matter how many kids and commitments you have, if there's passion you find the time. A couple of years ago they gave me six months' sabbatical, six whole months just for writing, and you know what? I put on ten pounds and spent most of the time wheeling the baby around the park. I didn't produce a single page. That's writing for you: when you make space for passion, it doesn't turn up. In the end I was desperate to get back to the job, just for a break from all the domestic business. But I learned a lesson there, that's for sure.

I looked at my watch: it was a fifteen-minute walk back to the apartment and I needed to go. I thought about what I ought to take for a boat trip, how hot or cold it would be and whether I should bring a book to read. Ryan was watching the waitress moving in and out of the shadows, proud and erect, the tresses of her hair hanging perfectly still. I put my things in my bag and moved to the edge of my seat, which seemed to catch his attention. He turned his head to me. What about yourself, he said, are you working on something?

## III

The apartment belonged to a woman called Clelia, who was out of Athens for the summer. It stood in a narrow street like a shady chasm, with the buildings rising to either side. On the corner opposite the entrance to Clelia's building was a café with a large awning and tables underneath, where there were always a few people sitting. The café had a long side window giving on to the narrow pavement, which was entirely obscured by a photograph of more people sitting outside at tables, so that a very convincing optical illusion was created. There was a woman with her head thrown back, laughing, as she raised her coffee cup to her lipsticked mouth, and a man leaning towards her across the table, tanned and handsome, his fingers resting lightly on her wrist, wearing the abashed smile of someone who has just said something amusing. This photograph was the first thing you saw when you came out of Clelia's building. The people in it were slightly larger than life-size, and always, for a moment, exiting the apartment, they seemed terrifyingly real. The sight of them momentarily overpowered one's own sense of reality, so that for a few disturbing seconds you believed that people were bigger and happier and more beautiful than you remembered them to be.

Clelia's apartment was on the top floor of the building and was reached by a curving marble staircase that passed the doors to the apartments on the other floors one by one. Three flights of stairs had to be climbed and three doors passed before Clelia's was reached. At the bottom the hallway was darker and cooler than the street, but because of the windows at the back of the upper storeys, as it rose it became lighter and warmer. Outside Clelia's door, just beneath the roof, the heat — with the strain of the climb up – was faintly stifling. Yet there was also the feeling of having accessed a place of privacy, because the marble staircase ended here and there was nowhere further to go. On the landing outside her door Clelia had placed a large sculpture made of driftwood, abstract in shape, and the presence of this object – where the landings on the lower floors were completely bare – confirmed that no one ever came up here who wasn't either Clelia or someone she knew. As well as the sculpture there was a cactus-like plant in a red earthenware pot, and a decoration – a charm made of woven strands of coloured material – hung from the pewter door knocker.

Clelia was a writer, apparently, and had offered her flat to the summer school for the use of the visiting writers, even though they were complete strangers to her. And in fact it was obvious, from certain features in her apartment, that she regarded writing as a profession worthy of the greatest trust and respect. To the right of the fireplace was a large opening through which Clelia's study could be accessed, a square secluded room whose large cherry-wood desk and leather swivel chair faced away from the single window. This room contained, as well as many books, several painted wooden models of boats, which had been mounted to the walls. They were very intricately and beautifully made, down to the miniature coils of rope and tiny brass instruments on their sanded decks, and the larger ones had white sails arranged in curving attitudes of such tension and complexity that it did indeed seem as though the wind was blowing in them. When you looked more closely, you saw that the sails were attached to countless tiny cords, so fine as to make them almost invisible, which had fixed them in these shapes. It required only a couple of steps to move from the impression of wind in the sails to the sight of the mesh of fine cords, a metaphor I felt sure Clelia had intended to illustrate the relationship between illusion and reality, though she did not perhaps expect her guests to go one step further, as I did, and reach out a hand to touch the white cloth, which was not cloth at all but paper, unexpectedly dry and brittle.

Clelia's kitchen was sufficiently functional to give the clear message that she didn't spend much time there: one of the cupboards was entirely filled with esoteric whiskies, another with relatively useless things – a fondue set, a fish kettle, a ravioli press – that were still in their boxes, and one or two were completely empty. If you left so much as a crumb on the counter-top, columns of ants would spring out from all directions and descend on it as though starved. The view from the kitchen window was of the backs of other buildings with their pipework and washing lines. The room itself was quite small and dark. Yet there was nothing you really needed that wasn't there.

In the sitting room Clelia's formidable collection of recordings of classical music could be found. Her hi-fi system consisted of a number of inscrutable black boxes, whose blankness and slenderness left one unprepared for the enormity of the sound they made. Clelia favoured symphonies: in fact, she possessed the complete symphonic works of all the major composers. There was a marked prejudice against compositions that glorified the solo voice or instrument, very little piano music and virtually no opera, with the exception of Janáček, of whose complete operatic œuvre Clelia had a boxed set. I wasn't sure I would choose to sit through symphony after symphony any more than I would spend the afternoon reading the *Encyclopaedia Britannica*, and it occurred to me that in Clelia's mind they perhaps represented the same thing, a sort of objectivity that arose when the focus became the sum of human parts and the individual was blotted out. It was, perhaps, a form of discipline, almost of asceticism, a temporary banishing of the self and its utterances – in any case, Clelia's symphonies in their serried ranks predominated. When you put one on, the apartment instantly seemed to grow ten times its actual size and to be accommodating a full orchestral assembly, brass, strings and all.

Clelia's bedrooms, of which there were two, were surprisingly spartan. They were small, box-like rooms, both of them painted pale blue. One of them contained bunk beds, the other a double bed. The bunk beds made it evident that Clelia had no children, for their presence, in a room that was not a child's room, seemed to suggest something that otherwise might have been forgotten. The bunk beds, in other words, stood for the concept of children generally rather than for any child specifically. In the other room, one entire wall was taken up with a set of mirrored wardrobes that I never looked inside.

In the centre of Clelia's apartment was a large light space, a hall, where the doors to all the other rooms converged. Here, standing on a plinth, was a glazed terracotta statue of a woman. It was large, around three feet tall – more if you included the plinth – and showed the woman in a striking attitude, her face lifted, her arms half raised with the palms and fingers open. She wore a primitive robe that had been painted white and her face was round and flat. Sometimes she looked as if she were about to say something, sometimes as if she were in despair. Occasionally she appeared to be conferring some kind of benediction. Her white garment glowed at dusk. You had to pass her frequently, going from one room to another, yet it was surprisingly easy to forget that she was there. Her white looming figure with its raised hands and its broad flat face, with its swiftly changing mood, was always slightly startling. Unlike the people in the café window downstairs, the terracotta woman made reality seem, for a moment, smaller and deeper, more private and harder to articulate.

The apartment had a large outdoor terrace that ran across the full width of the building's façade. From this terrace, high above the pavements, the surrounding rooftops with their baked, broken angles could be seen, and further away the smoggy distant hills of the suburbs. It faced, across the chasm of the street, the windows and terraces of the apartments opposite. Sometimes a face would appear at one or other of the windows. Once, a man came out on to his terrace and threw something over the side. A young woman came out after him and looked down over the railings at what he had thrown. Clelia's terrace was private and leafy, filled with big tangled plants in terracotta urns and hung with small glass lanterns: in the middle there was a long wooden table and many chairs, in which it could be imagined Clelia's friends and associates sat during the hot dark evenings. It was shaded by a huge vine in which, sitting one morning at the table, I noticed a nest. It was built into a fork amidst the tough, knotty stems. A bird was sitting in it, a pale grey dove: every time I looked, night or day, there she was. Her small pale head with its dark bead-like eyes moved around as though fretfully, yet for hour after hour she kept her vigil. Once I heard a great rustling overhead and looked up to see her clambering to her feet. She thrust her head through the canopy of leaves and gazed around her at the rooftops. Then with a snap of her wings she was gone. I watched her fly out over the street and then, circling, land on the rooftop opposite. She stayed there for a little while, calling, and then I watched her turn back and look at the place from which she had come. Having got this view of it, she opened her wings again and flew back, and with another great rustling and flapping overhead resumed her station.

I wandered around the apartment, looking at things. I opened a few cupboards and drawers. Everything was highly orderly. There was no confusion or secrecy: things were in their correct places and complete. There was a drawer for pens and stationery, a drawer for computer equipment, a drawer for maps and guides, a filing cabinet with papers in neat dividers. There was a first-aid drawer and a drawer for sellotape and glue. There was a cupboard for cleaning materials and another for tools. The drawers in the antique oriental bureau in the sitting room were empty and smelled of dust. I kept looking for something else, a clue, something rotting or breeding, a layer of mystery or chaos or shame, but I didn't find it. I wandered into the study and touched the brittle sails.

# IV

My neighbour from the plane was a good foot shorter than me and twice as wide: since I had got to know him sitting down, it was difficult to integrate these dimensions with his character. What located me was his extraordinary beak-like nose with the prominent brow jutting out above it, which gave him the slightly quizzical appearance of a seabird, crowned with his plume of silver-white hair. Even so it took me a moment to recognise him, standing in the shade of a doorway opposite the apartment building, dressed in buff-coloured knee-length shorts and a red checked shirt, immaculately ironed. There were various points of gold around his person, a fat signet ring on his little finger, a chunky gold watch, a pair of glasses on a gold chain around his neck and even a flash of gold when he smiled, all immediately noticeable, and yet I hadn't been aware of any of them during our conversation on the airplane the day before. That encounter had been, in a sense, immaterial: above the world, objects didn't count for so much, differences were less apparent. The material reality of my neighbour, which up there had seemed so light, was concretised down here, and the result was that he seemed more of a stranger, as though context were also a kind of imprisonment.

I was certain he saw me before I saw him, but he waited for me to wave before he acknowledged me in return. He looked nervous. He kept glancing up and down the street, where a fruit seller stood yelling inchoately beside a cart mounded with peaches and strawberries and chunks of watermelon that seemed to grin in the heat. His face took on an expression of pleased surprise when I crossed the road towards him. He kissed me slightly drily and fumblingly on the cheek.

'Did you sleep well?' he asked.

It was nearly lunchtime, and I had been out all morning, but it was apparent that he wished to create a sphere of intimacy in which our knowledge of one another was continuous and in which nothing had happened to me since we had said goodbye at the airport taxi rank the evening before. In fact I had slept very little in the small blue bedroom. There was a painting hanging on the wall opposite the bed, of a man in a trilby hat throwing back his head and laughing. When you looked you saw that he had no face, just a blank oval with the laughing void of his mouth in the middle. I kept waiting for his eyes and nose to become visible as the room got light, but they never did.

My neighbour said that his car was parked just around the corner and after a hesitation he placed his hand in the small of my back to guide me in the right direction. His hands were very large and slightly claw-like, and covered with white hair. He was concerned, he said, that I would not think much of his car. It had struck him that I might have imagined something far grander, and he was embarrassed if that was the case; but he himself didn't set much store by cars. And for driving around Athens, he had found that this was all he needed. But you could never tell, he said, what other people expected; he hoped I wouldn't be disappointed, that was all. We reached the car, which was small and clean and otherwise unremarkable, and got in. The boat, he said, was moored about forty minutes' drive away along the coast. He used to keep it at a marina much closer to the city, but the mooring was very expensive and so a couple of years ago he had decided to move it. I asked him where his house was, in relation to the centre, and he gestured vaguely with his hand toward the window and said that it was half an hour or so away over there.

We had pulled out on to the broad, six-lane avenue along which the traffic thundered ceaselessly through the city, where the heat and noise were extreme. The car windows were wide open, and my neighbour drove with one hand on the steering wheel while the other rested on the window sill so that his shirtsleeve flapped madly in the wind. He was an erratic driver, lunging from one lane to the next, and turning his head entirely away from the road while he talked, so that red lights and the backs of other cars would come rushing up to the windscreen before he noticed them. I was frightened and fell silent, staring out at the dusty lots and verges that had by now succeeded the big glinting buildings of the centre. We passed over an arching concrete intersection in a blare of horns and engine noise, the sun pounding on the windscreen and the smell of petrol and asphalt and sewage flooding through the open windows, and for a while drove alongside a man on a scooter, who had a little boy of five or six seated behind him. The boy was clinging to the man with both arms around his middle. He looked so small and unprotected, with the cars and metal palisades and huge junk-laden lorries rushing inches past his skin. He wore only shorts and a vest and flip-flops on his feet, and I looked through the window at his unshielded tender brown limbs and at his soft golden-brown hair rippling in the wind. Then the arching road curved around and began to descend, and there was the sea, blazing blue beyond a khaki-coloured scrubland littered with low abandoned buildings and unfinished roads and the skeletons of houses that had never been completed, where skinny trees now grew through the glassless windows.

I've been married three times, my neighbour said, as the little car flew down the hill towards the glittering water. He was aware, he said, that in yesterday's conversation he had only admitted to two, but he had come here today vowing to be honest. There had been three marriages, and three divorces. I'm the full disaster, he said. I was thinking about how to reply when he said that another thing he needed to mention was his son, who was presently living at the family house on the island and who was rather unwell. He was in an extremely anxious state, and had been calling his father all morning. Those calls would no doubt continue over the next few hours, and though he didn't want to answer them he would, of course, be obliged to. I asked what was wrong with his son and his birdlike face grew sombre. Was I familiar with the condition called schizophrenia? Well, that was what his son suffered from. He had developed it in his twenties after leaving university, and had been hospitalised several times over the past decade, but for a number of reasons too complicated to explain he was currently in his father's care. My neighbour had judged that he was safe enough on the island, so long as he didn't get his hands on any money. People were sympathetic there, and still held the family in sufficient esteem to tolerate small difficulties, of which there had already been a number. But a few days ago there had been a more serious episode, as a consequence of which my neighbour had had to ask the young man he had hired to be his son's companion on the island to keep him under, as it were, house arrest. His son couldn't bear incarceration, hence the constant phone calls, and when it wasn't his son phoning it was the companion, who felt that the job was exceeding the terms of his contract and wanted to renegotiate his salary.

I asked whether this was the same son his second wife had locked in the cellar, and he said that it was. He had been a sweet child, but then he had gone to university, in England as it happened, and had developed something of a drug habit. He left without completing his degree and came drifting back to Greece, where various attempts were made to find employment for him. He was living with his mother, on the large estate outside Athens she shared with her ski-instructor husband, and my neighbour didn't doubt that she found him a trial and a drag on her freedom, as his behaviour was deteriorating by the day; but all the same her first move, which was to have him committed without discussing it first with his father, was somewhat extreme. He was put on medication that made him so fat and inert he became, in effect, a vegetable; and his mother departed Athens with her husband, to take up their customary winter residence in the Alps. This was, of course, several years ago now, but the situation hadn't fundamentally changed. The boy's mother would have nothing more to do with him; if his father chose to remove him from hospital and have him live in the world, that was his responsibility.

I said it surprised me that his first wife, whom my neighbour had seemed rather to idealise in our earlier conversation, should behave with such coldness. It didn't seem to fit with the impression I had formed of her character. He considered this, and then said that she hadn't been like that in the time of their marriage: she had changed, had become a different person from the one that he knew. When he spoke of her fondly, it was the earlier version of herself he was speaking of. I said that I didn't believe people could change so completely, could evolve an unrecognisable morality; it was merely that that part of themselves had lain dormant, waiting to be evoked by circumstance. I said that I thought most of us didn't know how truly good or truly bad we were, and most of us would never be sufficiently tested to find out. But there must have been moments when he had glimpsed – even if only briefly – what she would become. No, he said, he didn't think there were: she had always been an excellent mother, devoted above everything else to the children. Their daughter had become a great success and had been awarded a scholarship at Harvard; subsequently she was poached by a global software firm and was now in Silicon Valley, a place I must surely have heard of. I said that I had, though I had always found it difficult to envisage; I could never establish to what degree it was conceptual, and to what degree an actual place. I asked whether he had ever visited her there; he admitted that he had not. He never found himself in that part of the world, and besides, he would be worried about leaving his son for the length of time such a visit would require. But it was true that he hadn't seen his daughter for several years, as she hadn't returned to Greece. It seems success takes you away from what you know, he said, while failure condemns you to it. I asked whether she had any children, and he said that she didn't. She was in a partnership – was that what you called it? – with another woman, and other than that her work was everything to her.

He supposed, he said, now that he thought about it, that his wife was something of a perfectionist. One argument, after all, was all it had taken to end their marriage: if there was a sign of what she might become, perhaps it was that failure was something she was unable to tolerate. After their separation, he said, she had immediately taken up with a very rich and notorious boyfriend, a ship-owner, a relative of Onassis: he was really fabulously wealthy, this man, and good-looking, and also a friend of her father, and my neighbour had never been able to find out why the relationship had ended, for it was his impression that this man was everything she had ever wanted. In a way it had helped him to understand the failure of their marriage, her choice of this handsome billionaire; he could accept his own defeat at the hands of such an adversary. Kurt the ski instructor, on the other hand, was baffling, a man without charm or money, a man who only came alive for a few months a year, when there was snow on the mountains; a man, moreover, of fanatical religious beliefs and observances, to which he apparently insisted his wife and her children – while they still remained at home – submit. The children told him tales, of enforced prayers and silences, of being made to sit at table – for hours if necessary – until they had finished every piece of food on their plates, of being asked to call him 'father' and forbidden television and entertainments on Sundays. Once my neighbour had had the temerity to ask her what she saw in Kurt and she replied, he is the exact opposite of you.

We were driving along by the water now, past scruffy-looking beaches where families were picnicking and swimming, past roadside shops selling parasols and snorkels and swimming costumes. My neighbour said that we were nearly there; he hoped I hadn't found the journey too long. He should mention, he said, lest I was expecting something grand, that his boat was quite small. He had owned it for twenty-five years, and it was steady as a rock in a gale, but it was of modest proportions. It had a small cabin where one person could comfortably spend the night, 'or two people,' he said, 'if they are very much in love'. He often spent the night there himself, and at certain times of year he would take the boat across to the island, a journey of three or four days. It was, in a sense, his hermitage, his place of solitude; he could motor just offshore, anchor it, and be completely alone.

At last we came in sight of the marina, and my neighbour pulled off the road and parked the car alongside a wooden pontoon where a line of boats were tied to their moorings. He asked me to wait there, while he went and bought some supplies. Also, he said, there were no facilities on the boat, so I should make myself comfortable before we left. I watched him walk back up toward the road and then I sat down on a bench in the sun to wait. The boats moved up and down in the bright water. Beyond them I could see the clear, crenellated shapes of the coast, and of a number of rocks and small islands that lay further out to sea, strung all across the bay. It was cooler here than in the city. The breeze made a dry, shuffling sound in the vegetation that stood in tangled clumps between the sea and the road. I looked at the boats, wondering which one belonged to my neighbour. They all seemed more or less alike. There were people around, mostly men of my neighbour's age, padding up and down the pontoon in deck shoes or working on their boats, their grizzled chests bare in the sun. Some of them stared at me, slack-jawed, their great ropy arms hanging by their sides. I took out my phone and dialled the number of the mortgage company in England, who were processing an application I had made just before I left for Athens to increase my loan. The woman who was dealing with the application was called Lydia. She had told me to call her today, but every time I tried I got her voicemail message. The message said that she would be out of the office on holiday until a date that had already passed, which gave the impression that she didn't listen to her voicemail very often. Sitting on the bench I got the message again, but this time – perhaps because I didn't have anything else to do – I left a message myself, saying that I had called as agreed and asking her to call me back. After this apparently pointless exercise, I looked around and saw that my neighbour was returning holding a carrier bag. He asked me to take it while he made the boat ready, and then he crossed the pontoon and getting down on his knees drew a length of sodden rope out of the water, with which he proceeded to pull the boat attached to the other end towards him. The boat was white, with wooden cladding and a bright blue canopy. There was a large black leather steering wheel at the front and an upholstered bench seat along the back. When it was close enough my neighbour hopped heavily on board and stretched out his hand for the carrier bag. For a while he busied himself stowing things away and then he held out his hand again to help me over. I was surprised to find myself not especially sure-footed in this exercise. I sat on the bench seat while he took the covers off the steering wheel and lowered the engine into the water and tied and untied numerous ropes, and then he stood at the wheel and started the engine, which made a watery growling sound, and we began to reverse slowly out of the marina.

We would drive for a while, my neighbour called above the noise of the engine, and when we reached a nice place he knew, we would stop and swim. He had removed his shirt, and his bare back faced me while he drove. It was very broad and fleshy, leathery with sun and age, and marked with numerous moles and scars and outcrops of coarse grey hair. Looking at it I felt overcome with a sadness that was partly confusion, as though his back were a foreign country I was lost in; or not lost but exiled, in as much as the feeling of being lost was not attended by the hope that I would eventually find something I recognised. His aged back seemed to maroon us both in our separate and untransfigurable histories. It struck me that some people might think I was stupid, to go out alone on a boat with a man I didn't know. But what other people thought was no longer of any help to me. Those thoughts only existed within certain structures, and I had definitively left those structures.

We were out by now in the open water, and my neighbour put the boat into a different gear so that it suddenly leaped forward, with such force that unnoticed by him I nearly fell over the back. The thunderous noise of the engine instantly displaced every other sight and sound. I grabbed the rail that ran along one side and clung on as we roared across the bay, the front of the boat rising and thumping down again repeatedly on to the water and a great spray fanning out to all sides. I felt angry that he hadn't warned me of what was about to happen. I couldn't move or speak: I could only cling on, my hair standing up on end and my face growing stiff with the pressure of wind. The boat thumped up and down and the sight of his bare back at the wheel made me angrier and angrier. There was a certain self-consciousness in the set of his shoulders: this was, then, a performance, a piece of showing off. He didn't once glance back at me, for people are at their least aware of others when demonstrating their own power over them. I wondered what he would have felt if he'd arrived at our destination to discover that I was no longer there; I imagined him explaining this latest piece of carelessness to the next woman he met on an airplane. She kept pestering me to go out on the boat, he would say, but it turned out she didn't know the first thing about sailing. To be perfectly honest, he would say, it was the full disaster: she fell overboard, and now I am very sad.

At last the sound of the engine died away; the boat slowed, and puttered towards a small rocky island that rose steeply out of the sea. My neighbour's phone rang and he looked quizzically at the screen before answering it. He began to speak mellifluously in Greek, pacing about the small deck and occasionally checking the steering wheel with a finger. I saw that we were approaching a clear little cove where many seabirds perched on the rocky promontories, and where the glittering water whirled and retreated against a tiny curl of sand. The island was too small to have anything human on it: it was untouched and deserted, except for the birds. I waited for my neighbour's conversation to conclude, which took a considerable amount of time. Eventually, though, he hung up. That was someone I haven't spoken to in many years, he said – in fact I was very surprised that she should call me. He was silent for a while, his finger on the steering wheel, his face sombre. She just heard about my brother's death, he continued, and she was calling to give her condolences. I asked when his brother had died. Oh, four, five years ago, he said. But she lives in the States and hasn't been back to Greece for a long time. She's here now on a visit, so she's only just got the news. His phone rang again almost immediately, and again he answered it. It was another Greek conversation, this one also lengthy but a little more businesslike. Work, he explained when it concluded, making a brushing gesture with his hand.

The boat drifted to a halt in the lapping water. He came to the back and opened a compartment, inside which lay a small anchor, and he hauled it by its chain over the side. This is a good place to swim, he said, if you would like to. I watched the anchor fall down through the clear water. When the boat was secured my neighbour stepped up on to the stern and dived heavily over the side. Once he had gone I wrapped a towel around myself and changed awkwardly into my swimming costume. Then I jumped in, swimming out in the opposite direction all the way to the perimeter of the island so that I could see the open sea beyond it. The other way, the distant shore was a bobbing line full of tiny shapes and figures. In the meantime another boat had arrived and was anchored not far from ours, and I could see the people sitting out on deck and hear the sound of their voices talking and laughing. They were a family group, with numerous children in bright costumes jumping in and out of the water, and now and again the sound of a baby wailing echoed thinly around the cove. My neighbour had got back on the boat and was standing there with his hand screening his eyes, watching my progress. It felt good to swim, after the tension of sitting still, of the heat of Athens and of spending time with strangers. The water was so clear and still and cool, and the shapes of the coastline so soft and ancient, with the little island nearby that seemed to belong to nobody. I felt that I could swim for miles, out into the ocean: a desire for freedom, an impulse to move, tugged at me as though it were a thread fastened to my chest. It was an impulse I knew well, and I had learned that it was not the summons from a larger world I used to believe it to be. It was simply a desire to escape from what I had. The thread led nowhere, except into ever expanding wastes of anonymity. I could swim out into the sea as far as I liked, if what I wanted was to drown. Yet this impulse, this desire to be free, was still compelling to me: I still, somehow, believed in it, despite having proved that everything about it was illusory. When I returned to the boat, my neighbour said he didn't like it when people swam too far out: it made him nervous; there were speedboats that could come out of nowhere, without warning, and such collisions were not un-heard of.

He offered me a Coke from the coldbox he kept on deck, and then proffered a box of tissues, from which he took a large handful himself. He blew his nose lengthily and thoroughly, while both of us watched the family on the neighbouring boat. There were two little boys and a girl playing there, shrieking as they leapt off the side and then clambering one after an-other back up the ladder, their bodies glittering with water. A woman in a sunhat sat on deck, reading a book, and beside her in the shade of the canopy was a baby's pram. A man in long shorts and sunglasses paced up and down the deck, speaking into his phone. I said that I found appearances more be-wildering and tormenting now than at any previous point in my life. It was as if I had lost some special capacity to filter my own perceptions, one that I had only become aware of once it was no longer there, like a missing pane of glass in a window that allows the wind and rain to come rushing through unchecked. In much the same way I felt exposed to what I saw, discomfited by it. I thought often of the chapter in *Wuthering Heights* where Heathcliff and Cathy stare from the dark garden through the windows of the Lintons' drawing room and watch the brightly lit family scene inside. What is fatal in that vision is its subjectivity: looking through the window the two of them see different things, Heathcliff what he fears and hates and Cathy what she desires and feels deprived of. But neither of them can see things as they really are. And likewise I was beginning to see my own fears and desires manifested outside myself, was beginning to see in other people's lives a commentary on my own. When I looked at the family on the boat, I saw a vision of what I no longer had: I saw something, in other words, that wasn't there. Those people were living in their moment, and though I could see it I could no more return to that moment than I could walk across the water that separated us. And of those two ways of living – living in the moment and living outside it – which was the more real?

Appearances, my neighbour replied, were highly valued in his own family, but he had learned –

perhaps fatally – to view them as a mechanism of deception and disguise. And it was in the closest relationships that the deception had to be greatest, for obvious reasons. He knew, for instance, that many of the men of his experience – his uncles, and people of their social circle – had a series of mistresses while remaining married to one woman all their lives. But it had never occurred to him that his father might have sustained his relationship to his mother in the same way. He perceived his father and mother as unitary while his uncle Theo, for instance, he knew to be duplicitous, though he wondered more and more whether that distinction had actually existed; whether, in other words, he had spent his adult life attempting to follow a template of marriage that had been, in fact, an illusion.

There had been a hotel Theo liked to stay in, not far from my neighbour's boarding school, and Theo would often call in and take him out to tea, always with a different 'friend' in tow. These friends were as scented and beautiful as aunt Irini was swarthy and squat; she had a number of warts on her face that sprouted coarse black hairs of an extraordinary girth and length, and my neighbour had been mesmerised his whole life by this feature, which was still real to him though Irini had been dead for thirty years and which symbolised the enduring nature of repulsion, while beauty was seen once and never seen again. When Irini died, at the age of eighty-four after sixty-three years of marriage, uncle Theo refused to allow her to be buried and instead had her encased in glass and kept in the vaults of a Greek chapel in Enfield, where he visited her every day of the six months that remained to him. My neighbour had never kept company with Theo and Irini without witnessing scenes of the most extraordinary violence: even a telephone call to the house usually involved an argument, with one of them picking up the extension to abuse the other while the caller played referee. His own parents, though fiercely combative, never approached the heights of Theo and his wife – theirs was a colder though perhaps a bitterer war. It was his father who died first, in London, and his body was stored in the same vault where Irini had lain, for his mother had taken it into her head to commission the construction of a family tomb back on the island, an undertaking so grandiose that it had fallen well behind schedule and was not ready to receive him when he died. She had conceived this idea when his father first fell ill, and the last year of his father's life was spent receiving almost daily bulletins on the progress of the tomb being built to envelop him. This unique method of torture might have seemed to be the conclusive move in their lifelong argument, but in fact when his mother herself came to die – a year to the day, as he believed he had already told me, after his father – the tomb was still not finished. She joined her husband in the vault in Enfield, and it wasn't until several months later that their bodies were flown together back to the island on which both of them had been born. It had fallen to my neighbour to oversee the interring, and also the exhumation of other family members – his grandparents on both sides, numerous uncles and aunts – from their places in the cemetery and their relocation in the enormous new tomb. He flew back, with his parents' corpses in the hold, and spent all day immersed with the gravediggers in the grisly business of transporting and arranging the various coffins. He was particularly unnerved to witness the return to the earth's surface of his grandfather, his mother's father, who had been a man of great mischief and the cause – to the end of their days – of many of his parents' arguments, for the power even in memory that he continued to hold over his daughter. In the late afternoon, his parents were the last to be lowered into the vast marble structure. My neighbour had a taxi waiting to take him back to the airport, as he was due to return to London straight away. But midway through the journey, sitting in the taxi, a terrible realisation struck him. In all the rearranging of the family bodies, he had somehow failed to place his parents side by side: worse still, he distinctly re-called, there in the back of the taxi, that it was his grandfather's coffin that lay between the two. Imme-diately he ordered the taxi driver to turn around and take him back to the cemetery. As they approached, he told the taxi driver that he would have to help him, for by now it was nearly dark and everyone else would have gone home. The taxi driver agreed, but no sooner had they entered the cemetery gates in the darkness than he took fright and ran away, leaving my neighbour alone. He did not recall, my neigh-bour said, quite how he managed to unseal the tomb single-handed: he was still a fairly young man, but even so he must have been endowed in that mo-ment with a superhuman strength. He climbed over the edge and descended into the tomb and there, sure enough, he saw his parents' two coffins with the grandfather between them. It was not so hard to slide them into their proper positions, but once he'd done it he realised that owing to the steepness and depth of the tomb it was going to be impossible for him to get out again. He called and shouted, to no avail; he leapt and scrabbled at the smooth sides of the tomb, trying to find a foothold.

But I suppose I must have got out somehow, he said, because I certainly didn't spend all night there, though I thought I might have to. Perhaps the taxi driver came back after all – I don't remember. He smiled, and for a while the two of us watched the family on the other boat, across the bright water. I said that when my sons were the ages of those two leaping boys, they were so intimate it would have been hard to disentangle their separate natures. They used to play together without pause from the moment they opened their eyes in the morning to the moment they closed them again. Their play was a kind of shared trance in which they created whole imaginary worlds, and they were forever involved in games and projects whose planning and execution were as real to them as they were invisible to everyone else: sometimes I would move or throw away some apparently inconsequential item, only to be told that it was a sacred prop in the ongoing make-believe, a narrative which seemed to run like a magic river through our household, inexhaustible, and which they could exit and re-enter at will, moving over that threshold which no one else could see into another element. And then one day the river dried up: their shared world of imagination ceased, and the reason was that one of them – I can't even recall which one it was – stopped believing in it. In other words, it was nobody's fault; but all the same it was brought home to me how much of what was beautiful in their lives was the result of a shared vision of

80

things that strictly speaking could not have been said to exist.

I suppose, I said, it is one definition of love, the belief in something that only the two of you can see, and in this case it proved to be an impermanent basis for living. Without their shared story, the two children began to argue, and where their playing had taken them away from the world, making them unreachable sometimes for hours at a time, their arguments brought them constantly back to it. They would come to me or to their father, seeking intervention and justice; they began to set greater store by facts, by what had been done and said, and to build the case for themselves and against one another. It was hard, I said, not to see this transposition from love to factuality as the mirror of other things that were happening in our household at the time. What was striking was the sheer negative capability of their former intimacy: it was as though everything that had been inside was moved outside, piece by piece, like furniture being taken out of a house and put on the pavement. There seemed to be so much of it, because what had been invisible was now visible; what had been useful was now redundant. Their antagonism was in exact proportion to their former harmony, but where the harmony had been timeless and weightless, the antagonism occupied

81

space and time. The intangible became solid, the visionary was embodied, the private became public: when peace becomes war, when love turns to hatred, something is born into the world, a force of pure mortality. If love is what is held to make us immortal, hatred is the reverse. And what is astonishing is how much detail it gathers to itself, so that nothing remains untouched by it. They were struggling to free themselves from one another, yet the very last thing they could do was leave one another alone. They fought over everything, disputed ownership of the most inconsequential item, were enraged by the merest nuance of speech, and when finally they were maddened by detail they erupted into physical violence, hitting and scratching one another; which of course returned them to the madness of detail again, because physical violence entails the long-drawn-out processes of justice and the law. The story of who had done what to whom had to be told, and the matters of guilt and punishment established, though this never satisfied them either; in fact it made things worse, because it seemed to promise a resolution that never came. The more its intricacies were specified, the bigger and realer their argument grew. Each of them wanted more than anything to be declared right, and the other wrong, but it was impossible to assign blame entirely to either of them. And I realised eventually, I said, that it could never be resolved, not so long as the aim was to establish the truth, for there was no single truth any more, that was the point. There was no longer a shared vision, a shared reality even. Each of them saw things now solely from his own perspective: there was only point of view.

My neighbour was silent for a while. Presently he said that in his case his children had been his mainstay, through all the ups and downs of his marital career. He had always felt himself to be a good father: he supposed, in fact, that he had been more able to love his children and feel loved by them in return than he had their various mothers. But his own mother had once said to him, in the period after his first marriage had ended when he was deeply concerned about the effect the divorce was having on the children, that family life was bittersweet no matter what you did. If it wasn't divorce it would be something else, she said. There was no such thing as an unblemished childhood, though people will do everything they can to convince you otherwise. There was no such thing as a life without pain. And as for divorce, even if you lived like a saint you would still experience all the same losses, however much you tried to explain them away. I could weep just to think that I'll never see you again as you were at the age of six – I would give anything, she said, to meet that six-year-old one more time. But everything falls away, try as you might to stop it. And for whatever returns to you, be grateful. So he has tried to be grateful, even for his son, who has failed so spectacularly to survive out in the world. His son had become, like so many vulnerable people, obsessed with animals, and my neighbour had involved himself in more headaches than he could possibly recount by giving in to the unceasing requests that this or that helpless creature be rescued and given a home. Dogs, cats, hedgehogs, birds, even once a baby lamb half-killed by a fox, into whose mouth my neighbour had sat up a whole night spooning warm milk. During that vigil, he said, he had willed the lamb to live, not especially for its own sake but for the affirmation this would have provided of the lonely route he had chosen in relation to his son, which was to treat him with the utmost sensitivity and indulgence. Had the lamb lived, it might have constituted a kind of approval – if only from the universe – of my neighbour's decision to act in direct contradiction to the boy's mother, who would have abandoned him to a mental hospital. But of course he found himself burying the thing the next morning, while Takis was still asleep; and this was just one of countless incidents whereby he had come to feel foolish for deciding to treat the child without resort to cruelty. It seems, he said, that the universe favours those like his ex-wife, who disown that which reflects badly on them; though in stories, of course, the bad things return to haunt them. His current problems stemmed from an evening last week, when his son's companion had closeted himself away to work on his Ph.D. and Takis had stolen out under cover of darkness, and taken it upon himself to attempt the liberation of numerous anilmals kept in fenced enclosures on the island, including an eccentric sort of menagerie being raised as a pet project by a local entrepreneur, so that now there were a number of exotic beasts – ostriches, llamas, tapirs, and even a herd of tiny ponies no bigger than dogs – roaming loose across the island. Their owner was a newcomer, less respectful of the family's ancestry, and was very angry at the damage to his property and his livestock: in his eyes Takis was a hooligan, a criminal, and there wasn't a great deal my neighbour could say or do in his defence. You learn very quickly, he said, that your children are exempt only from your own judgement. If the world finds them wanting, you have to take them back. Though this, of course, is something he supposes he has always known, for his mentally disabled brother, now a man in his early seventies, has never even left the place where he was born.

He asked whether I would like to swim again before we returned to the mainland and this time I remained within sight of the two boats and swam close to the cove, where the baby's cries echoed among the high rocks. The father was pacing up and down the deck with the little body clasped to his shoulder and the mother was fanning herself with her book while the three children sat at her feet cross-legged. The boat was hung with pale cloths and draperies to provide shade and the breeze occasionally sent them billowing in and back out again, so that the group was hidden briefly from view and then revealed once more. They held their positions, waiting, I could see, for the baby to stop crying, for the moment to release them and for the world to move forward again. On the other side of the cove my neighbour had swum out in a short straight furrow and immediately returned, and I watched him climb up the small ladder back on to the boat. He moved around the deck in the distance with his slightly rolling gait, towelling his fleshy back. A few feet away from me a black cormorant stood perched on a rock, staring motionless out to sea. The baby stopped crying and the family immediately began to stir, changing their positions in the confined space as though they were little clockwork figures rotating on a jewellery box; the father bending and putting the child in its pram, the mother rising and turning, the two boys and the girl straightening their legs and joining their hands so that they made a pinwheel shape, their bodies glittering and flashing in the sun. I suddenly felt afraid, alone in the water, and I returned to the boat, where my neighbour was packing things away and opening the compartment in readiness to bring up the anchor. He suggested I lie down on the bench seat, as I was probably tired, and try to sleep while he drove across to the mainland. He gave me a kind of shawl to cover myself with, and I drew it up all the way over my head, so that the sky and the sun and the dancing water were blotted out; and this time, when the boat made its surging leap forward amid the deafening noise of the engine, I experienced it as a kind of comfort and found that I did go into a half-sleep. Occasionally I would open my eyes and see the unfamiliar cloth just in front of them and then I would close them again; and feeling my body being borne blindly through space I had the sense of everything in my life having become atomised, all its elements separated as though an explosion had sent them flying away from the centre in different directions. I thought of my children and wondered where they were at this moment. The image of the family on the boat, the bright rotating circle on the jewellery box, so mechanically and fixedly constellated and yet so graceful and correct, turned behind my eyes. I was reminded, with extraordinary clarity, of lying half-asleep as a child on the back seat of my parents' car on the interminable winding journey home from the seaside, where we often drove for the day during the summer. There was no direct road between the two places, just a rambling network of country lanes that looked on the map like the tangled illustrations of veins and capillaries in a textbook, so that it made no particular difference which way you went as long as it was generally in the right direction. Yet my father had a route he preferred, because it seemed to him to be marginally more direct than the others, and so we always went the same way, crossing and recrossing the alternative roads and passing signposts to places we had either already been through or would never see, my father's notion of the journey having established itself over time as an insurmountable reality, to the extent that it would have seemed wrong to have found ourselves passing through those unknown villages, though in fact it would have made no difference at all. We children would lie on the back seat, drowsy and nauseous with the swaying motion, and sometimes I would open my eyes and see the summer landscape passing through the dusty windows, so full and ripe at that time of year that it seemed impossible it could ever be broken down and turned to winter.

The hurtling motion of the boat began to slow and the sound of the motor to die away. My neighbour asked me courteously, when I sat up, whether I had managed to switch off for a while. We were drawing close to the marina, its white boats startling against their background of blue, and beyond them the brown roadscape, desultory in the heat, all of it seeming to move unstoppably up and down in the sunshine though in fact the motion was ours. If I was hungry, my neighbour said, there was a place he knew just over there that made souvlaki. Had I eaten souvlaki before? It was very simple but could be very good. If I would just be patient while he moored the boat and went through the necessary procedures, we could be eating shortly, and afterwards he would drive me back to Athens.

# V

In the evening I was meeting an old friend of mine, Paniotis, at a restaurant in the centre of town. He called to give me directions, and also to tell me that someone else – a woman novelist I might have heard of – would probably be joining us. She had been very insistent; he hoped I didn't mind. She wasn't a person he cared to offend: I've been in Athens too long, he said. He described the route meticulously, twice. He was being kept in a meeting, he said, otherwise he would have come to fetch me himself. He didn't like leaving me to find my way on my own but he hoped he had made things sufficiently clear. If I counted the traffic lights as he had told me to, turning right between the sixth and the seventh, I would not go wrong.

At evening, with the sun no longer overhead, the air developed a kind of viscosity in which time seemed to stand very still and the labyrinth of the city, no longer bisected by light and shade and unstirred by the afternoon breezes, appeared suspended

in a kind of dream, paused in an atmosphere of extraordinary pallor and thickness. At some point darkness fell, but otherwise the evenings were strangely
without the sense of progression: it didn't get cooler,
or quieter, or emptier of people; the roar of talk and
laughter came unstaunched from the glaring terraces
of restaurants, the traffic was a swarming, honking
river of lights, small children rode their bicycles along
the pavements under the bile-coloured streetlamps.
Despite the darkness it was eternal day, the pigeons
still scuffling in the neon-lit squares, the kiosks open
on street corners, the smell of pastry still hanging in
the exhausted air around the bakeries. In Paniotis's
restaurant a fat man in a heavy tweed suit sat alone at
a corner table, delicately cutting a slice of pink watermelon into small pieces with his knife and fork and
placing them carefully in his mouth. I waited, looking around the dark-panelled interior with its insets
of bevelled glass, where the sea of empty tables and
chairs was multiply reflected. This was not, Paniotis
acknowledged when he arrived, a fashionable place;
Angeliki, who intended to join us presently, would
certainly be displeased, but at least it was possible to
talk here, and one could be sure of not meeting anyone one knew who could interrupt. I probably didn't
share his feelings – he hoped, really, that I didn't –
but he was no longer interested in socialising; in fact,

increasingly he found other people positively bewildering. The interesting ones are like islands, he said: you don't bump into them on the street or at a party, you have to know where they are and go to them by arrangement.

He asked me to stand up so that he could embrace me, and when I came out from behind the table he looked closely into my eyes. He had been trying to remember, he said, how long it was since our last encounter – did I know? It must have been more than three years ago, I said, and he nodded his head as I spoke. We had lunch in a restaurant in Earls Court, on a day that had been hot by English standards, and for some reason my children and husband had come too. We were on our way somewhere else: we stopped to meet Paniotis, who was in London for the book fair. I went away from that lunch, he said, feeling that my own life had been a failure. You seemed so happy with your family, so complete, it was an image of how things ought to be.

His body, when we hugged, felt extremely light and fragile. He was wearing a threadbare lilac-coloured shirt, and a pair of jeans that hung from him in folds. He drew back and looked at me closely again. There is something of the cartoon character about Paniotis's face: everything about it is exaggerated, the cheeks very gaunt, the forehead very high, the eyebrows winging off like exclamation marks, the hair flying out in all directions, so that one has the curious feeling one is looking at an illustration of Paniotis rather than at Paniotis himself. Even when he is relaxed he wears the expression of someone who has just been told something extraordinary, or who has opened a door and been very surprised by what he has found behind it. His eyes, within this rictus-like expression, are very mobile and changeable and often bulge dramatically forward, as though one day they might fly out of his face altogether with astonishment at what they have witnessed.

And now, he said, I can see that something has happened, and I have to say I would not have expected it. I do not understand it at all. That day, he said, in the restaurant, I took a photograph of you with your family – do you remember? Yes, I said, I remembered. I said that I hoped he wasn't about to show the photograph to me and he looked sombre. If you don't wish it, he said. But of course I have brought it with me; it's here in my briefcase. I told him that his taking a photograph was, in fact, the thing that stood out in my mind from that day. I remembered thinking that it was an unusual thing to do, or at least a thing I would not have thought to do myself. It marked some difference between him and me, in that he was observing something while I, evidently, was entirely immersed in being it. It was one of those moments, I said, that in retrospect have come to seem prophetic to me. And indeed, being so immersed, I did not notice that Paniotis went away from our encounter feeling that his life had been a failure, any more than the mountain notices the climber that loses his footing and falls down one of its ravines. Sometimes it has seemed to me that life is a series of punishments for such moments of unawareness, that one forges one's own destiny by what one doesn't notice or feel compassion for; that what you don't know and don't make the effort to understand will become the very thing you are forced into knowledge of. While I spoke Paniotis looked more and more aghast. That is a terrible notion that only a Catholic could have come up with, he said. Though I can't say there aren't quite a few people I would like to see punished in so delightfully cruel a fashion. Those are the ones, however, who are certain to remain unenlightened by suffering to the end of their days. They make sure of it, he said, picking up the menu and turning with a lifted finger to the waiter, an immense grey-bearded man clad in a long white apron, who all this time had been entrenched so absolutely motionless in the corner of the almost empty room that I hadn't noticed him. He came and stood before our table with his powerful arms folded across his chest, nodding his head while Paniotis spoke rapidly to him.

That day in London, Paniotis resumed, turning back to face me, I realised that my little dream of a publishing house was destined to remain just that, a fantasy, and in fact what that realisation caused me to feel was not so much disappointment at the situation as astonishment at the fantasy itself. It seemed incredible to me that at the age of fifty-one I was still capable of producing, in all innocence, a completely unrealisable hope. The human capacity for self-delusion is apparently infinite – and if that is the case, how are we ever meant to know, except by existing in a state of absolute pessimism, that once again we are fooling ourselves? I had thought there was nothing, having lived my whole life in this tragic country, about which I could any longer deceive myself, but as you have so unhappily pointed out, it is the very thing you don't see, the thing you take for granted, that deceives you. And how can you even know you have taken something for granted until it is no longer there?

The waiter loomed beside us carrying several dishes, and Paniotis broke off with a final pantomimed gesture of dismay, leaning back to let him put things on the table. There was a carafe of pale yellow wine, a dish of tiny green olives on their stalks that looked bitter but tasted sweet and delicious, and a plate of cold, delicate mussels in their black shells.

To fortify us, Paniotis said, for the arrival of Angeliki. You will find that Angeliki has become very grand, he said, since one of her novels won some prize or another somewhere in Europe and she is now considered – or at least considers herself – to be a literary celebrity. Her sufferings – whatever they were – being over she has elected herself a sort of spokesperson for suffering womanhood generally, not just in Greece but in other territories that have demonstrated an interest in her work. Wherever she is asked to go, she goes. The novel, he said, concerns a woman painter whose artistic life is gradually being stifled by her domestic arrangements: her husband is a diplomat, and the family is always being uprooted and moved to a new place, so that the woman painter comes to feel that her own work is merely decorative, a pastime, while her husband's is considered not just by him but by the world to be important, to forge events rather than simply provide a commentary on them, and that when there is a conflict between the two – which, this being a novel by Angeliki, there often is – his needs triumph over hers. And eventually her work starts to become mechanical, a pretence; there is no passion, yet her urge to express herself remains. In Berlin, where the family are now living, she meets a young man, a painter, who reignites her passion, for painting and for everything else – but now

96

the problem is that she feels too old for this young man, and also she feels miserably guilty, especially about her children, who have sensed that something is wrong and have started to become upset. Most of all she feels angry with her husband, for putting her in this position, for causing her to lose her passion in the first place and leaving her entirely respons- ible for the consequences. And the young painter is still making her feel old, with his all-night parties and his recreational drugs and his wonder at the marks experience has left on her woman's body. There is no one she can talk to, no one she can tell – what a lonely place, smirks Paniotis. That's the title, by the way: *A Lonely Place*. My argument with An- geliki, he says, concerns her substitution of painting for writing, as if the two were interchangeable. The book is obviously about herself, he says, and yet she knows nothing at all about painting. In my experi- ence painters are far less conventional than writers. Writers need to hide in bourgeois life like ticks need to hide in an animal's fur: the deeper they're buried the better. I don't believe in her painter, he says, making the children's packed lunches in her state-of- the-art German kitchen while fantasising about sex with a young muscled androgyne in a leather jacket.

I asked him what it was, in London, that had caused him to lose faith in his publishing house, which he had only just launched and which indeed shortly afterwards – I had heard – was taken over by a large corporation, so that Paniotis was now a company editor rather than the director of his own enterprise. My reverence for all things English, he said after a silence, his sorrowful eyes brimming and rolling in their sockets, was not reciprocated. This was when things had started to get difficult here, he continued, though no one guessed then how much worse they would become. The publishing house was to be devoted exclusively to translating and printing English-language authors unheard of in Greece, writers the commercial publishers wouldn't touch, whose work Paniotis deeply admired and was determined to make available for his countrymen. But at a particular moment he was unable to provide the advance payments to these authors, many of whose books he had translated himself to cut costs. In London he found himself excoriated, even by the writers themselves, for non-payment of money that the books, strictly speaking, had not yet actually earned; he was treated with the greatest disdain by everyone, was threatened with legal action, and worst of all came away with the impression that these writers he had worshipped as the artists of our time were in fact cold and unempathetic people devoted to self-promotion and above all else, to money. He had made it quite clear to them that if he was forced to pay, his publishing house would collapse before it had even begun, which indeed is what happened; those same writers are regularly rejected by the company he works for now, who are interested only in turning out best-sellers. And so I learned, he said, that it is impossible to improve things, and that good people are just as responsible for it as bad, and that improvement itself is perhaps a mere personal fantasy, as lonely in its way as Angeliki's lonely place. We are all addicted to it, he said, removing a single mussel from its shell with his trembling fingers and putting it in his mouth, the story of improvement, to the extent that it has commandeered our deepest sense of reality. It has even infected the novel, though perhaps now the novel is infecting us back again, so that we expect of our lives what we've come to expect of our books; but this sense of life as a progression is something I want no more of.

In his marriage, he now realised, the principle of progress was always at work, in the acquiring of houses, possessions, cars, the drive towards higher social status, more travel, a wider circle of friends, even the production of children felt like an obligatory calling-point on the mad journey; and it was inevitable, he now saw, that once there were no more things to add or improve on, no more goals to achieve or stages to pass through, the journey would seem to have run its course, and he and his wife would be beset by a great sense of futility and by the feeling of some malady, which was really only the feeling of stillness after a life of too much motion, such as sailors experience when they walk on dry land after too long at sea, but which to both of them signified that they were no longer in love. If only we had had the sense, he said, to make our peace with one another then, to start from the honest proposition that we were two people not in love who nonetheless meant one another no harm; well, he said, his eyes brimming again, if that had been the case I believe we might have learned truly to love one another and to love ourselves. But instead we saw it as another opportunity for progress, saw the journey unfolding once more, only this time it was a journey through destruction and war, for which both of us demonstrated just as much energy and aptitude as always.

These days, he said, I live very simply. In the mornings, at sunrise, I drive to a place I know twenty minutes outside Athens and I swim all the way across the bay and all the way back again. In the evenings I sit on my balcony and I write. He closed his eyes briefly and smiled. I asked him what it was he was writing, and his smile widened. He said, I am writing about my childhood. I was so happy as a child, he continued, and I realised a little while ago that there was nothing I wanted so much as to recall it piece by piece, with every possible detail. The world that happiness existed in has completely disappeared, not just in my own life but in Greece as a whole, for whether it knows it or not Greece is a country that is on its knees and dying a slow and agonising death. In my own case, I sometimes wonder whether it was the very happiness of my childhood that has meant I have had to be taught how to suffer. I seem to have been exceptionally slow to understand where pain comes from, and how it comes. It has taken me a long time to learn to avoid it. I read in the newspaper the other day, he said, about a boy with a curious mental disorder which compels him to seek physical risk and therefore injury wherever possible. This boy is forever putting his hand in the fire, and throwing himself off walls, and climbing trees in order to fall out of them; he has broken nearly every bone in his body, and of course is covered in cuts and bruises, and the newspaper asked his poor parents for their comment on the situation. The problem is, they said, he has no fear. But it seems to me that exactly the reverse is true: he has too much fear, so much that he is driven to enact the thing of which he is afraid, lest it should happen of its own accord. I think that if I had known, as a child, what was possible in terms of pain, I might have had much the same response. You might remember in the *Odyssey*, he said, the character of Elpenor, Odysseus's crewmate who falls off the roof of Circe's house because he is so happy he forgets he has to use a ladder to come down. Odysseus encounters him in Hades later on, and he asks him why on earth he died in such a foolish manner. Paniotis smiled. I always found that a charming detail, he said.

A woman who was certain to be Angeliki – since there were no other diners, and no one else had entered the restaurant in all this time – had come in and was interrogating the waiter quite energetically; a conversation of inexplicable length ensued, in the course of which the two of them went outside and shortly after came back again, whereupon it continued more energetically than ever, the woman's tawny well-cut hair swishing with the rapid movements of her head and her lovely grey dress – made of a flimsy silk material – swirling as she shifted from one foot to another, impatient as a stamping pony. She wore striking high-heeled sandals of silver leather and carried a matching bag, and would have been the picture of elegance had she not, when she turned around to look in the direction of the waiter's pointing arm – and seen at the end of it our table – disclosed a face so extraordinarily anxious that anyone looking at it could only feel anxious too on her behalf. As Paniotis had predicted, Angeliki was chagrinned by his choice of restaurant; she had only come in here in the first place, she said, to ask for directions to the venue Paniotis had chosen, not realising that this was it, and the waiter had had to take her outside and show her the sign to convince her; and even then she felt sure that a more suitable place must be trading under the same name nearby. But I chose it specially for you, Paniotis said, his eyes bulging. The chef is from your home town, Angeliki; all your favourite Baltic dishes are on the menu. Please excuse him, Angeliki said, placing a manicured hand on my arm. She then remonstrated rapidly with Paniotis in Greek, a tirade that ended with him excusing himself from the table and disappearing off towards the toilets.

I'm so sorry I couldn't be here earlier, Angeliki continued breathlessly. I had to attend a reception, and then return home to put my son to bed – I haven't seen all that much of him lately, as I've been on tour with my book. It was a tour of Poland, she added before I could ask, mainly in Warsaw but I visited other cities too. She asked whether I had ever been to Poland and when I said that I had not, she nodded her head a little sadly. The publishers there can't afford to invite many writers to come, she said, and it is a pity,

103

because they need writers there in a way that people here do not. In the past year, she said, I have visited many places for the first time, or for the first time in my own right, but Poland was the tour that affected me the most, because it made me see my books not just as entertainments for the middle classes but as something vital, a lifeline in many cases, for people – largely women, it has to be admitted – who feel very much alone in their daily lives.

Angeliki picked up the carafe and melancholically poured herself a teaspoon of wine, before filling my glass almost to the brim.

'My husband is a diplomat,' she said, 'so we have travelled a lot, evidently, for his work. But it feels completely different to be travelling for my work, and to be travelling independently. I admit that I have sometimes felt afraid, even in places I'm quite familiar with. And in Poland I was very nervous, because there was very little there – including the language – that I recognised. But some of it, at first, was down to the plain fact that I was unused to being by myself. For instance,' she continued, 'we lived in Berlin for six years, but even going there alone, as a writer, it seemed somehow alien. Partly it was be-cause I was seeing a new aspect of the city – the literary culture, which I was absolutely outside of be-fore – and partly because being there without my husband caused me to feel, in an entirely new way, what I actually am.'

I replied that I wasn't sure it was possible, in marriage, to know what you actually were, or indeed to separate what you were from what you had become through the other person. I thought the whole idea of a 'real' self might be illusory. you might feel, in other words, as though there were some separate, autonomous self within you, but perhaps that self didn't actually exist. My mother once admitted, I said, that she used to be desperate for us to leave the house for school, but that once we'd gone she had no idea what to do with herself and wished that we would come back. And she still, even now that her children were adults, would conclude our visits quite forcefully and usher us all off to our own homes, as though something terrible would have happened if we had stayed. Yet I was quite sure that she experienced that same sense of loss after we'd gone, and wondered what she was looking for and why she had driven us away in order to look for it. Angeliki began to rummage in her elegant silver bag and presently pulled out a notepad and pencil.

'Please excuse me,' she said. 'I just need to write that down.' She sat writing for a moment and then glanced up and said, 'Could you just repeat the second part?'

I noticed that her notepad was very orderly, like the rest of her appearance, the pages neatly written in straight lines. Her pencil was made of silver too, with a retractable lead which she screwed firmly back into its casing. When she had finished she said: 'I have to admit that I was astonished by the response in Poland, really very surprised. You know, I presume, that the women of Poland are highly politicised: my audiences were ninety per cent women,' she said, 'and they were very vocal. Of course, Greek women are vocal too —'

'But they are better dressed,' said Paniotis, who had by now returned. To my surprise, Angeliki took this interjection seriously.

'Yes,' she said, 'the women in Greece like to be beautiful. But in Poland I felt this to be a disadvantage. The women there are so pale and serious: they have wide, flat, cool faces, though their skin is often bad, presumably because of the weather and their diet, which is appalling. And their teeth,' she added with a little grimace, 'are not good. But they have a seriousness I envied, as though they had not been distracted, were never distracted from the reality of their own lives. I spent a lot of time in Warsaw with a woman journalist,' she went on, 'a person of about my own age and also a mother, who was so thin and flat and hard I found it difficult to believe she was a woman at all. She had straight mouse-coloured hair that went all the way down her back, and a face as white and bony as a glacier, and she wore big workman's jeans and big clumsy shoes, and she was as clear and sharp and beautiful as an icicle. She and her husband alternated strictly every six months, one working and the other looking after the children. Sometimes he complained, but so far he had accepted the arrangement. But she admitted to me, proudly, that when she went away for work, which she often did, the children would sleep with her photograph beneath their pillows. I laughed,' Angeliki said, 'and told her I felt sure my son would die rather than be caught sleeping with a photograph of me beneath his pillow. And Olga gave me such a look that I suddenly wondered whether even our children were infected with the cynicism of our gender politics.'

Angeliki's face had a softness, almost a mistiness, that was attractive while also being the reason for its careworn appearance. It seemed that anything could leave an impression in that softness. She had the small, neat features of a child, yet her skin was creased as though by worry, which gave her a look of frowning innocence, like a pretty little girl that has not got her way.

'Talking to this journalist,' she continued, 'whose name as I have mentioned was Olga, I wondered whether my whole existence – even my feminism – had been a compromise. I felt it had lacked seriousness. Even my writing has been treated as a kind of hobby. I wondered whether I would have had the courage to be like her, for there seemed to be so little pleasure in her life, so little beauty – the sheer physical ugliness of that part of the world is astonishing – that I wasn't sure, under similar circumstances, whether I would have had the energy to care. That was why I was surprised by the numbers of women who attended my readings – it almost seemed as though my work was more important to them than it is to me!'

The waiter came to take our order, which was a lengthy process, as Angeliki appeared to be discussing each item on the menu in turn, asking numerous questions as she moved down the list which the waiter answered gravely and sometimes lengthily, never becoming the slightest bit impatient. Paniotis sat beside her, rolling his eyes and occasionally remonstrating with the pair of them, which only served to make the process even longer. Finally it seemed to be concluded and the waiter moved heavily and slowly away, but then Angeliki summoned him back with a little intake of breath and a lifting of her finger, having had, apparently, a few afterthoughts. Her doctor had put her on a special diet, she said to me once he had departed for the second time and vanished through the mahogany louvred doors at the far end of the restaurant, since she had become unwell on her return to Greece from Berlin. She had found herself overwhelmed by the most extraordinary lethargy and – it didn't trouble her to admit it – by sadness, which she had supposed to be a sort of cumulative physical and emotional exhaustion from so many years abroad, and had spent six months more or less incapacitated in bed; months in which she had discovered, she said, that her husband and son could manage without her far better than she might have imagined, so that when she got up again and returned to normal life she found that her role in the household had diminished. Her husband and son had become used to doing much of what had been her work around the house – or to having it left undone, she said – and in fact had evolved new habits of their own, many of which she disliked; but she recognised, at that moment, that she was being given a choice, and that if she wanted to escape her old identity then this was her opportunity. For some women, she said, it would be the realisation of their greatest fear, to discover that they were not needed, but for her it had had the opposite effect. She found, too, that illness had enabled her to view her life, and the people in it, with greater objectivity. She realised that she was not so bound up with them as she had thought, particularly with her son, on whose account she had always, from the moment of his birth, suffered an immense preoccupation, seeing him as uniquely sensitive and vulnerable, to the extent that she was unable – she now realised – to leave him alone even for a minute. Returning to the world after her illness, her son seemed if not quite a stranger to her then less painfully connected to her by every filament. She still loved him, of course, but she no longer saw him and his life as something she needed to resolve into perfection.

'For many women,' she said, 'having a child is their central experience of creativity, and yet the child will never remain a created object; unless,' she said, 'the mother's sacrifice of herself is absolute, which mine never could have been, and which no woman's ought to be these days. My own mother lived through me in a way that was completely uncritical,' she said, 'and the consequence was that I came into adulthood unprepared for life, because nobody saw me as important in the way she did, which was the way I was used to being seen. And then you meet a man who thinks you're important enough to marry you, so it seems right that you should say yes. But it is when you have a baby that the feeling of importance really returns,' she said, with growing passion, 'except that one day you realise that all this – the house, the husband, the child – isn't importance after all, in fact it is the exact opposite: you have become a slave, obliterated!' She paused dramatically, her face lifted, her hands flat on the table top amidst the silverware. 'The only hope,' she continued more quietly, 'is to make your child and your husband so important in your own mind that your ego has enough sustenance to stay alive. But in fact,' she said, 'as Simone de Beauvoir observes, such a woman is nothing but a parasite, a parasite on her husband, a parasite on her child.'

'In Berlin,' she continued after a while, 'my son attended an expensive private college, paid for by the embassy, where we met a great number of rich and well-connected people. The women were of a kind I had never known before in my life: nearly all of them worked in a profession – doctors, lawyers, accountants – and most of them had a large number of children, five or six apiece, whose lives they supervised with amazing diligence and energy, running their families like successful corporations on top of the demanding careers most of them already had. Not only that, these women were as well groomed and well turned out as could be: they went to the gym every day, ran marathons for charity, were as thin and wiry as greyhounds and always wore the most expensive, elegant clothes, though their sinewy muscular bodies were often curiously sexless. They went to church, baked the cakes for the school fete, chaired the debating society, held dinner parties at which six courses were served, read all the latest novels, attended concerts, played tennis and volleyball at the weekends. One such woman would have been enough,' she said, 'but in Berlin I met quantities of them. And the funny thing was, I could never remember their names, or their husbands' names either: in fact,' she said, 'I don't recall a single one of their faces, or the faces of any of their families, except for the face of one child, a boy of about my son's age, who was terribly disabled and went around in a kind of motorised cart which had a shelf for his chin to rest on, so that his head – which otherwise I suppose would have fallen forward on to his chest – was always propped up.' She paused, troubled, as though seeing the boy's face before her once more. 'I don't remember his mother', she continued, 'ever complaining about her lot: on the contrary, she was a tireless fundraiser for charities supporting his condition, on top of all the other things she had to do.

'Sometimes,' she said, 'I almost wonder whether the exhaustion I felt when we returned from Berlin was in fact the collective exhaustion of these women, which they refused to feel themselves and so had passed on to me. One always seemed to see them running: they ran everywhere, to work and back again, to the supermarket, in groups around the park – talking together as easily as if they were standing still – and if they had to stop for a traffic light they would keep running on the spot in their enormous white shoes until it changed and they could progress again. The rest of the time they wore flat shoes with rubber soles, supremely practical and supremely ugly. Their shoes were the only inelegant thing about them,' she said, 'yet I felt they were the key to the whole mystery of their nature, for they were the shoes of a woman without vanity.

'I myself,' she continued, extending her silvered foot out from beneath the table, 'developed a weakness for delicate shoes when we returned to Greece. Perhaps it was because I had begun to see the virtues of standing still. And for the character in my novel, shoes like these represent something forbidden. They are the sort of thing she would never wear. Moreover, when she does see women wearing such shoes, it makes her feel sad. She has believed, until now, that this was because she found such women pitiful, but in fact when she thinks about it honestly it is because she feels excluded or disbarred from the concept of womanhood the shoes represent. She feels, almost, as if she isn't a woman at all. But if she isn't a woman, what is she? She is experiencing a crisis of femininity that is also a creative crisis, yet she has always sought to separate the two things in the belief that they were mutually exclusive, that the one disqualified the other. She looks out of the window of her apartment at the women running in the park, always running, and she asks herself whether they are running towards something or away from it. If she looks long enough she sees that they are simply running around in circles.'

Bearing an enormous silver tray the waiter approached. He unloaded the dishes one after the other and placed them on the table. Having taken such trouble with the ordering of the food, Angeliki served herself only minuscule amounts, her forehead furrowed with frowns as she prodded her spoon into each one. Paniotis arranged a selection of things on my plate, explaining to me what they were. He said that he had last come to this restaurant on the eve of his daughter's departure to America, when likewise he had not wished to be interrupted by acquaintances, of which, at this point, he had far too many in Athens. Sharing the food, they had reminisced about a holiday they once took along the coast north of Thessaloniki, from where many of these dishes originated. He held up the spoon and asked Angeliki whether she wouldn't take a little more, but she half closed her eyes and inclined her head in reply, like a saint patiently refusing temptation. And you, he said to me, you have very little also. I explained that I had eaten souvlaki for lunch. Paniotis grimaced, and Angeliki wrinkled her nose.

'Souvlaki is very greasy,' she said. 'Along with their indolence,' she added, 'it is the reason why the Greeks are so fat.'

I asked Paniotis how long ago it was that he had travelled north with his daughter, and he said that it was very shortly after he and his wife had divorced. In fact it was the first time he had taken his children anywhere on his own. He remembered that in the car, driving out of Athens and into the hills, he had kept glancing at them on the back seat in the rearview mirror, feeling as wrongful as if he were kidnapping them. He expected them, at any minute, to discover his crime and demand their immediate return to Athens and their mother, but they did not: in fact, they made no comment on the situation at all, not during all the long hours of a journey in which Paniotis felt himself to be getting further and further away from everything trusted and known, everything familiar, and most of all from the whole security of the home he had made with his wife, which of course no longer even existed. Yet moving geographically away from this scene of loss felt unbearable, just as

115

sometimes, said Paniotis, people cannot bear to go away from the place where a loved one has died.

'I kept waiting for the children to ask to go home,' he said, 'but in fact it was I who wanted to go home: I began to realise, in the car, that as far as they were concerned they *were* home, at least partly, because they were with me.'

That, he said, was the loneliest of realisations; and it was not helped by their arrival at the hotel where they were due to break their journey for the night, which was a most terrible place in a scruffy, windswept seaside town where a giant apartment complex had been half built and then abandoned, so that everywhere there were huge piles of sand and cement and great stacks of breeze blocks, as well as large pieces of machinery that appeared to have been simply left there mid-job, diggers with shovels of earth half raised, forklift trucks with pallets still suspended on their outstretched prongs, all frozen in situ like prehistoric monsters drowned in silt, while the building itself, an aborted embryo in a still-fresh swirl of tarmac, stood in all its spectral madness, staring with its glassless windows out to sea. Their hotel was filthy and full of mosquitoes, and there was cement grit between the sheets, and it amazed him to see his children bouncing and laughing on the ugly metal beds with their garish nylon covers, for up until now –

116

sometimes by arrangement but often by mere chance – he and his wife had only ever taken them to places of beauty and comfort, and as well as being filled with the dreadful conviction that his life from here on was going to be as luckless as the previous life had been fortunate, he felt the most terrible pity for the children themselves. He had booked one room for the three of them and eventually he got them to bed, but lay awake for many hours himself, sandwiched between them: 'never,' Paniotis said, 'have I found a night as hard to get through as that one. And in the morning, however it came, we saw that the weather was bad, as it can sometimes be along that coast at Easter. It was already raining very hard, and was so windy on the shore, where the hotel looked out, that the spume was lifted from the water and blew away in great desolate sweeps that looked like phantoms crossing the sky. We should have stayed where we were, but I was so determined to get away that I put the children back in the car and started to drive with the rain hammering on the roof, hardly able to see where I was going. At points the road had been turned literally to mud, and as we climbed back up into the hills above the coast I saw there was an actual danger it might be washed away. On top of that, the children had been bitten very badly by mosquitoes during the night and had scratched the bites, some of which looked like they might become infected. So I needed to find a pharmacy, but in all the drama of the rain I must have taken a wrong turning, because instead of joining the motorway the road became steeper and steeper and narrower and narrower and the hills more and more desolate, until I saw that we were in a veritable mountain range, with enormous dizzying drops to each side and great wads of cloud around the peaks. The storm had caused herds of goats and mountain pigs to run madly over the mountainsides, and sometimes they came swarming across the road right in front of the car; and then, a little further on, the road was deluged from above by a river that had burst its banks and the children screamed as the water poured through one of the windows that had been left slightly open. The sky was so black by now that even though it was only late morning it was as if night had fallen; but up ahead, through the rain, I suddenly saw a building where there were lights. Amazingly enough, it was a mountain inn, just beside the road, and we pulled over straight away, jumping out of the car and running across to the entrance of the low stone building with our jackets over our heads and flinging open the door. It was a nice enough place, in fact, and we must have looked quite extraordinary to the people inside, the children covered in bleeding bites, all three of us unkempt and soaking wet. The main room was full of girl scouts, at least thirty of them, all wearing a uniform that consisted of a navy skirt and blouse, a navy beret and a knotted yellow tie. They were singing all together, a song in French, with one or two of them accompanying on small musical instruments. This bizarre scene seemed quite acceptable to me, after the awful seaside town and the storm and the mad goats; and in fact one of the things that happened to me on that holiday, and that I believe has not changed since, was that I began to feel for the first time that I was seeing what was really there, without asking myself whether or not I was expecting to see it. When I think back to the time before, and especially to the years of my marriage, it seems to me as though my wife and I looked at the world through a long lens of preconception, by which we held ourselves at some unbreachable distance from what was around us, a distance that constituted a kind of safety but also created a space for illusion. We never, I think, discovered the true nature of the things we saw, any more than we were ever in danger of being affected by them; we peered at them, at people and places, like people on a ship peer at the passing mainland, and should we have seen them in any kind of trouble, or they us, there would have been nothing whatever either one of us could have done about it.

119

'It may have been to say something of this sort that I suddenly felt an overpowering need to talk to my wife, and I asked the owner of the inn if she had a telephone I could use. The girl scouts – who were part of a religious organisation of a kind I believe is quite common in France, and who told us they were on a walking tour of the area – had meanwhile made room on the benches around the large wooden table at which they sat and had cheerfully resumed their singing while the rain came down in torrents outside. The woman showed me the telephone, and asked if I would like her to make some hot chocolate for the children. She also produced, in her kindness, a tube of disinfectant cream for their bites. In the telephone booth I dialled the number of my wife's new apartment in Athens, and was surprised to hear a man answer the phone. When eventually I got Chrysta on the line I told her everything about our predicament, said that we were lost somewhere in the mountains, that there was a terrible storm, that the children were frightened and covered in mosquito bites and that I doubted my ability to cope in such a crisis. But instead of responding with sympathy and concern, she was absolutely silent. The silence was only a few seconds long, but in that period, while she failed to come in on time and to take up, as it were, her part in our lifelong duet, I understood, completely and definitively, that Chrysta and I were no longer married, and that the war we were embroiled in was not merely a bitterer version of the same lifelong engagement, but was something far more evil, something that had destruction, annihilation, non-existence as its ambition. Most of all it wanted silence: and this, I realised, was what my conversations with Chrysta were all leading towards, a silence that would in the end remain unbroken, though on this occasion she did break it. I'm sure you'll manage somehow, was what she said. And shortly after, the conversation concluded.

'Returning to my children after this exchange,' Paniotis said, 'I felt the most extraordinary sense of insecurity, almost like vertigo. I remember clutching the wooden edge of the table for what seemed like the longest time, while all around me the girl scouts sang. But then, after a while, I felt a distinct warmth at my back and looked up to see that great yellow beams of sunlight were coming through the leaded windows. The girl scouts rose from their chairs and packed away their instruments. The storm had passed; the innkeeper opened the door to let the sunshine through. And out we all went into the dripping, sparkling world, where I stood with my children beside the car, my whole body shaking, and watched the troop of scouts marching off down the road, whistling, until they disappeared from view. What struck me most about that sight was that they did not, evidently, consider themselves to be lost, and nor did they find anything frightening in the turn the weather had taken or even in the proclivities of the mountains themselves. They did not take any of these things personally. That was the difference between them and me, and at that time it was all the difference in the world.

'My daughter reminded me,' he said, 'on that last evening we spent here, of the walk we took later that day. She did not, in fact, remember the hotel or the storm or even the girl scouts, but she did remember our descent into the Lousios gorge, which we decided to make when we passed a sign on the road pointing down to it. There was a monastery along the gorge I had long wanted to visit, and so she and my son and I left the car by the side of the road and set off down the path. She remembered our walk down there in the sunshine beside plunging waterfalls, and the wild orchids she picked along the way, and the monastery itself, perched on the edge of an extraordinary ravine, where she was asked to put on one of the ugly long skirts made of old curtains they kept in mothballs in a basket by the door before they would permit her to enter. If there was anything traumatic about that day, she told me, it was having to put on that horrible smelly skirt. On the way back up,' Paniotis said, 'the sun grew so hot, and our bites began to itch so unbearably, that the three of us tore off our clothes and leaped into one of the deep pools the waterfall had made, despite the fact that it was quite close to the path and that we could have been seen at any minute by passers-by. How cold the water was, and how incredibly deep and refreshing and clear – we drifted around and around, with the sun on our faces and our bodies hanging like three white roots beneath the water. I can see us there still,' he said, 'for those were moments so intense that in a way we will be living them always, while other things are completely forgotten. Yet there is no particular story attached to them,' he said, 'despite their place in the story I have just told you. That time spent swimming in the pool beneath the waterfall belongs nowhere: it is part of no sequence of events, it is only itself, in a way that nothing in our life before as a family was ever itself, because it was always leading to the next thing and the next, was always contributing to our story of who we were. Once Chrysta and I divorced, things did not join up in that way any more, although I tried for years to make it seem as though they did. But there was no sequel to that time in the pool, nor ever will be. And so my daughter has gone to America,' he said, 'like her brother before her, both of them getting as far away from their parents as they possibly can. And of course I'm sad,' he said, 'but I can't pretend I don't think they've done the right thing.'

'Paniotis,' Angeliki exclaimed, 'what are you saying? That your children emigrated because their parents got divorced? My friend, I'm afraid you're mistaken in thinking you're that important. Children leave or children stay depending on their ambitions: their lives are their own. Somehow we've become convinced that if we say even a word out of place we've marked them forever, but of course that is ridiculous, and in any case, why should their lives be perfect? It is our own idea of perfection that plagues us, and it is rooted in our own desires. For instance my mother thinks that the greatest misfortune is to be an only child. She simply cannot accept that my son will not have brothers and sisters, and I'm afraid I've given her the impression that this situation has not come about by choice, as a way of avoiding talking to her about it all the time. But she's always telling me about this doctor or that doctor she's just heard of, who can work miracles; the other day she sent me a newspaper clipping about a Greek woman who had a baby at the age of fifty-three, with a note telling me not to give up hope. Yet for my husband it is completely normal that our son should grow up alone, because he was an only child himself. And for me, of course, it would be disastrous to have more children: I would be completely submerged, as so many women are. I ask myself why it is my mother wishes to see me submerged in my turn, when I have important work to do, when it would not be in my best interests and would be, as I say, tantamount to disaster, and the answer is that her desire is not about me but about herself. I'm sure she wouldn't wish me to consider myself a failure for not being the mother of six children, yet that is precisely what her behaviour could cause me to feel.

'The parts of life that are suffocating', Angeliki said, 'are so often the parts that are the projection of our parents' own desires. One's existence as a wife and a mother, for example, is something often walked into without question, as though we are propelled by something outside ourselves; while a woman's creativity, the thing she doubts and is always sacrificing for the sake of these other things – when she wouldn't dream, for instance, of sacrificing the interests of her husband or son – has been her own idea, her own inner compulsion. While I was in Poland,' she said, 'I vowed to develop a less sentimental view of life, and if there is something I regret in my novel, it is that the material circumstances of the characters are so comfortable. It would be a more serious book, I believe, if that were not the case. Spending time with

Olga,' she said, 'certain things came to light for me, as objects under water come to light when the water drains away. I realised that our whole sense of life as a romance – even our conception of love itself – was a vision in which material things played far too great a role, and that without those things we might find that certain feelings diminished while others became accentuated. I was very attracted to the hardness of Olga,' she said, 'to the hardness of her life. When she spoke about her relationship with her husband it was as though she were speaking about the parts of an engine, explaining how they worked or did not work. There was no romance in it, no place that was covered up and that you weren't allowed to see. And so I was not jealous of the husband at all, but when she spoke about her children, about the photograph of her they kept beneath their pillows, I realised I felt angry, as I used to feel angry with my sisters and my brother when our mother gave her attention to them. I was jealous of Olga's children; I didn't want them to love her in that way, to exert that power over her. I started to feel more sympathetic towards the husband, being treated like a car engine; and then she told me that for a period of time he had left, had left the family, unable to bear this lack of sentimentality any longer, and had gone and lived in a flat on his own. When he returned, they resumed their life as

126

before. Was she not angry with him, I said, for deserting her and leaving her to take care of the children alone? No, on the contrary, she was pleased to see him. We are completely honest with one another, she said, and so I knew when he came back that it was because he had accepted the way things were. I tried to imagine,' Angeliki said, 'what this marriage was like, in which nobody had to make promises or apologise, in which you didn't have to buy flowers for the other person or cook them a special meal or light the candles to make a flattering atmosphere, or book a holiday to help you get over your problems; or rather, in which you were made to do without those things and live together so honestly and nakedly. And still I kept coming back to the children, and to the photograph they kept beneath the pillow, because it suggested that after all Olga was guilty of sentimentality, was capable of romance, only it was a romance of mother and child – and if she was capable of that, then why not everything? I admitted to her that I was jealous of her children, whom I had never even met, and she said to me, it is obvious, Angeliki, that you have never grown up and that this is how you are able to be a writer. Believe me, Olga said, you are very fortunate: I watched my daughter grow up from one day to the next when her father went away. She became, Olga said, in that period, extremely hostile to men: Olga recalled taking her one day around an art gallery in Warsaw, and when they arrived at a religious painting of Salome holding the severed head of John the Baptist, the child had cheered. On another occasion, Olga reprimanded her for some disparaging remark concerning the opposite sex, and her daughter had said that she didn't see why it was necessary that men exist. There don't need to be men, she had said, there only need to be mothers and children. Olga conceded that she was partly responsible for her daughter's perception of things, but the plain truth was that she would never have left the children in the way their father had, though undoubtedly he loved them; but she herself simply wouldn't have been capable of it, and whether that difference was a biological fact or merely a consequence of conditioning, it still had to be accounted for. You would do the same, Olga said to me, if it ever came to it.' Angeliki paused. 'I said that on the contrary, I believed my son belonged more to his father than he did to me. But she refused to accept that that could ever be the case, unless I had an unusual degree of respect for male authority. At that I had to laugh: the idea of me, of all people, nurturing an undue respect for male authority! But I have thought a great deal about that remark since,' Angeliki said, 'for obvious reasons. In my novel, the character is compromised by her desire to be free on the one hand and her guilt about her children on the other. All she wishes is for her life to be integrated, to be one thing, rather than an eternal series of oppositions that confound her whichever way she looks. One answer, of course, is that she divert her passion to her children, where it will do no harm; and that is the answer, ultimately, that she chooses. Yet it is not what I feel myself,' Angeliki said, rearranging the lovely grey tissue of her sleeves.

The waiter loomed beside our table; the restaurant was apparently closing now, and Angeliki rose, looking at her little silver watch and saying that she had enjoyed herself so much she had entirely lost track of the time. She had to be up early in the morning, for a television interview; 'but it was such a pleasure', she said, holding out her hand to me, 'to meet you. I think Paniotis would have preferred to have you to himself, but I'm afraid I insisted, since you were here, on my right to take part. I will treasure our conversation,' she said, squeezing my fingertips; 'perhaps we can meet again and continue it, woman to woman, the next time I am in London.'

She opened her bag and took out a little card with her details on, which she handed to me; with a swirl of her dress and a flicker of her silver heels she was gone, and I saw her face passing briefly outside the window, set once more in its striking configuration of frowning lines, which brightened when she caught my eye through the glass and raised her hand in farewell.

'If I may I will walk with you,' Paniotis said, 'as far as your apartment.'

As we set off down the dark, hot pavement towards the main road with its throbbing lights and unceasing sound of traffic, he told me that Angeliki was angry with him, because he was editing an anthology of Greek writing from which her work had been omitted.

'Vanity', he said, 'is the curse of our culture; or perhaps it is simply my own persistent refusal', he said, 'to believe that artists are also human beings.'

I said that in fact I had liked Angeliki, though she appeared to have forgotten that we had met before, at a reading I gave several years ago in Athens where she and her husband were among the audience. Paniotis laughed.

'That was another Angeliki,' he said, 'an Angeliki who no longer exists and has been written out of the history books. Angeliki the famous writer, the feminist of international renown, has never met you before in her life.'

When we reached the entrance to my apartment building, Paniotis looked at the larger-than-life figures in the darkness of the café window, the woman still laughing, the man still crinkling his eyes at her in all his handsome false modesty.

'At least they're happy,' he said. He opened his briefcase and took out an envelope and pressed it into my hand. 'It remains your truth,' he said, 'whatever has happened. Don't be afraid to look at it.'

# VI

It was a curious group – a mixed bag, as Ryan had put it. Watch out for the kid with the Demis Roussos hair and the bumfluff, he said, he simply won't shut up.

The room was small and grey, but it had large windows overlooking Kolonaki Square, a concrete enclosure where people sat reading newspapers on benches in the shade of plane trees with graffitied concrete bases. The hot spaces were already deserted at ten o'clock in the morning. Pigeons advanced in their circling, tatty formations across the paving slabs with their heads down, pecking.

The students were discussing whether the windows should be open or shut, for the room was morbidly cold and no one had been able to work out how to turn down the air conditioning. There was also the question of whether the door should be open or closed, the lights on or off, and whether the computer, which was projecting a blank blue rectangle on to the wall and making a humming noise, would be needed or could be closed down. I had already noticed the boy Ryan mentioned, who had a great shock of black curly hair that flowed down over his shoulders, and a nascent moustache of slightly paler hair nestling on his upper lip. Of the others it was hard at first to get any sense at all. There seemed to be a roughly equal number of men and women, but no two of them shared any characteristic of age, dress or social type. They had taken their places around a large white Formica table that was really a number of smaller tables pushed together to form a square. There was an atmosphere of uncertainty, almost of unease, in the anonymous room. I reminded myself that these people wanted something from me: that though they didn't know me, or one another, they had come here with the purpose of being recognised.

It was decided that the windows should be opened but the door shut, and the person nearest to each side got up to do so. Ryan's boy observed that it did seem odd to be opening the windows to warm *up* a room, but that science had involved us in many such inversions of reality, some of which were more useful than others. We should accept occasionally being inconvenienced by our conveniences, he said, just as we had to tolerate flaws in our loved ones: nothing was ever perfect, he said. Many of his fellow Greeks, he continued, believed that air conditioning was severely deleterious to health, and there was now a nationwide movement to keep it switched off in offices and public buildings, a sort of back-to-nature idea which was itself perfectionism of a kind, though it meant that everybody got very hot; which, he concluded somewhat delightedly, could only result in air conditioning being invented all over again.

I took a piece of paper and a pen and drew the shape of the large square table at which we all sat. I asked them for their names, of which there were ten in all, and wrote each one down in their place around the square. Then I asked each of them to tell me something they had noticed on their way here. There was a long, shuffling silence of transition; people cleared their throats, rearranged the papers in front of them or gazed blankly into space. Then a young woman, whose name, according to my diagram, was Sylvia, began to speak, having glanced around the room apparently to ascertain that no one else was going to take the initiative. Her small, resigned smile made it clear that she often found herself in this position.

'When I was getting off the train,' she said, 'I noticed a man standing on the platform with a small white dog on his shoulder. He himself was very tall and dark,' she added, 'and the dog was quite beautiful. Its coat was curly and as white as snow, and it sat on the man's shoulder and looked around itself.'

Another silence ensued. Presently a man of very neat and diminutive appearance – Theo, according to my diagram – who had come formally dressed in a pinstriped suit, put up his hand to speak.

'This morning,' he said, 'I was crossing the square opposite my apartment building, on my way to the metro, and I saw on one of the low concrete walls around the square a woman's handbag. It was a large and very expensive-looking handbag,' he said, 'made of the shiniest black patent leather with a gold clasp at the top, and it was standing there quite open on the wall. I looked around for a person likely to own such a thing, but the square was deserted. I wondered then whether the owner had been robbed, and the handbag left there while its contents had been stolen, but when I approached and looked inside – for the clasp was undone and the top was wide open, and I could examine the interior without touching it – I saw that everything was still there, a leather wallet, a set of keys, a powder compact and lipstick, even an apple that was presumably intended for a snack during the day. I stood there for quite a while, waiting to see who would turn up, and when nobody did I walked to the metro after all, because I had seen that otherwise I would be late. But I realised, while I was walking, that I should have taken the bag to a police station.'

Theo stopped, his story apparently at an end. The others immediately flew at him with a volley of questions. Having realised he should have handed the bag in to the police, why didn't he turn around and go back? If he was late, why had he not simply handed the bag in at a nearby shop or even a kiosk, for safe keeping, or at the very least told a passer-by about the situation? He could even have taken the bag with him, and made the necessary calls at a more convenient time – better that than just to leave it there, for anyone to steal! Theo sat through this interrogation with his arms folded across his chest, a benign expression on his small, neat face. After a considerable length of time, when the questions had died down, he spoke again.

'I had just crossed the square,' he said, 'and had turned around, in that moment having had this thought about the police, when what should I see but a young policeman, exactly halfway between myself and the bag, which I could still see sitting on the wall along the far side. He was coming up the path, at the end of which you must turn in one of two directions: right, which would have brought him to me, or left, which would take him straight to the bag. If he turned right, I saw that I would have no choice but to inform him, and to embroil myself in all the paperwork and wasted time that such acts entail. Fortunately for me,' Theo said, 'he turned left, and I stood there long enough to see him reach the bag, look around himself for its owner and peer inside at its contents as I had done, and then pick it up and take it with him on his way.'

The group applauded this performance heartily, while Theo continued to smile benignly in their midst. It was interesting to consider, said the long-haired boy – Georgeou, as my diagram now told me – that a story might merely be a series of events we believe ourselves to be involved in, but on which we have absolutely no influence at all. He himself had noticed nothing on his journey here: he habitually did not notice things which did not concern him, for that very reason, that he saw the tendency to fiction-alise our own experiences as positively dangerous, because it convinced us that human life had some kind of design and that we were more significant than we actually were. As for him, his father had driven him here: they had had a very interesting conversa-tion on the way about string theory, and then he had got out and come upstairs to this room.

'It is surely not true,' the girl sitting next to him said, with an expression of perplexity, 'that there is no story of life; that one's own existence doesn't have a distinct form that has begun and will one day end, that has its own themes and events and cast of characters.' She herself, on the way here, had passed an open window from which had drifted the sound of someone practising the piano. The building, it so happened, was a music college of the kind she herself had left two years before, abandoning her lifelong hopes of becoming a professional musician; she recognised the piece as the D minor fugue from Bach's *French Suites*, a piece she had always loved and that caused her, hearing it so unexpectedly, to feel there on the pavement the most extraordinary sense of loss. It was as though the music had once belonged to her and now no longer did; as though she had been excluded from its beauty, was being forced to see it in the possession of someone else, and to revisit in its entirety her own sadness at her inability, for a number of reasons, to remain in that world. Certainly another person, she said, passing that window and hearing the D minor fugue, would have felt something completely different. In itself, the music coming out of the window means nothing at all, and whatever the feelings that might be attached to it, none of them had caused the music to be played in the first place, or the window to be left open so that the sound of it could be heard by passers-by. And even a person observing these events, she said, from across the road, could not have guessed, simply by seeing and hearing, what the story really was. What they would have seen was a girl walking past, at the same time as hearing some music being played from inside a building.

'Which in fact', Georgeou responded, his finger lifted in the air and a wild grin appearing on his face, 'is all that actually happened!'

The girl – her name, when I looked, was Clio – was perhaps in her late twenties, but she had a child-like appearance, her dark hair drawn straight back into a ponytail and her pale, sallow skin bare of make-up. She wore a sleeveless kind of tunic, which added to her air of simplicity. I could imagine her in the monasticism of a practice room, her fingers flying surprisingly across the black and white keys. She looked at Georgeou with a face entirely passive and still, clearly in the expectation that he would have a great deal more to say.

Thankfully, Georgeou continued, there was an infinite thing called possibility, and an equally useful thing called probability. We had an excellent piece of evidence in terms of the music college, a place the majority of people would understand to be in the business of turning out professional musicians. Most people would have some concept of what a professional musician was, and would understand that the possibility of failure in such a profession was as great as the possibility of success. Hearing the music coming out of the building, therefore, they could envisage the person playing it as one who was running this risk, and whose fate could therefore take one of two basic forms, both imaginable by the average person.

'In other words,' Georgeou said, 'I could deduce your story from the facts alone, and from my own experience of life, which is all that I know for a certainty, most importantly in this case my experience of failure, such as my failure to memorise the constellations of the southern hemisphere, which never ceases to upset me.' He folded his hands and looked at them with a downcast expression.

I asked Georgeou how old he was, and he replied that he had turned fifteen last week. His father had bought him, as a birthday gift, a telescope, which they had set up on the flat roof of their apartment building and through which he was now able to study the sky, and most particularly the phases of the moon, in which he had a special interest. I said that I was glad he had received such a satisfying present, but that it was perhaps time to listen to what the others had to say. He nodded his head, his face brightening. He just wished to add, he said, that he was familiar with the D minor fugue from the *French Suites*: his father had played him a recording of it, and personally he had always found it to be quite an optimistic piece of music.

At this, the person sitting next to him began to speak.

'Music,' she said, in a languorous and dreamlike manner. 'Music is a betrayer of secrets; it is more treacherous even than dreams, which at least have the virtue of being private.'

The woman who said this was of a glorious though eccentric appearance, somewhere in her fifties, with a demolished beauty she bore quite regally. The bones of her face were so impressively structured as to verge on the grotesque, an impression she had chosen to accentuate – in a way that struck me as distinctly and intentionally humorous – by surrounding her already enormous blue eyes in oceans of exotic blue and green shadow and then drawing, not carefully, around the lids with an even brighter blue; her sharp cheekbones wore slashes of pink blusher, and her mouth, which was unusually fleshy and pouting, was richly and inaccurately slathered in red lipstick. She wore a great quantity of gold jewellery and a dress, also blue, of gathered chiffon that left her neck and arms exposed, where the skin was very brown and intricately creased. Her name, according to my chart, was Marielle.

'For example,' she continued after a long pause, her enormous blue eyes travelling the faces around her, 'it was when I heard my husband singing

"L'amour est un oiseau rebelle" in the shower that I realised he was being unfaithful to me.' She paused again, closing her fleshy lips together with difficulty over her distinctly large and protuberant front teeth as though to moisten them. 'He was of course singing the part of Carmen herself,' she resumed, 'though I don't think he realised his mistake, or would even have cared had he known. He has always been lazy about details, since he is a person of extremes, and prefers not to be detained by facts. As far as he was concerned he was simply singing out of sheer joy, so good was it to be him in our apartment on that sunny morning, with his mistress tucked away somewhere on the other side of town while he showered in his stall of travertine and gold, where he even likes to keep a few hardier artworks, as well as a small piece of the Parthenon frieze that is still presumed to be missing and that he uses as a soap dish; with the new high-pressure hot-water system we had just had installed and the towels he had ordered all the way from Saks Fifth Avenue in New York, which enveloped you like a baby in its mother's arms and made you want to go back to sleep again.

'I myself was in the kitchen,' she said, 'squeezing oranges. I had just made myself the most delicious breakfast, with the ripest little melon I had found in the market and a slice of fresh cheese I bought from a woman who keeps beautiful goats on a hillside near Delphi, when I heard the sound of him singing. I knew immediately what it meant. The idiot, I thought – why does he have to holler it out so that I can hear it all the way in the kitchen? I, the only one who knows what could have caused that soap opera of betrayal to pop into his head, taking for himself the best part, just as he would always take the best part of whatever was on my plate, simply reach across and take whatever he liked the look of, even though I had saved it until last. Why couldn't he have kept his mouth shut? And all before I had had the chance to eat my beautiful breakfast, which now he would find waiting for him untouched on the counter when he came out of the shower: his happiness, I knew, would be complete.'

She paused to tuck a strand of hair, which was dyed a bright yellow blonde, behind her ear, and moistened her lips again before she resumed. 'This morning,' she said, 'I had arranged to call in at his office on my way here, to discuss financial matters, about which in any case we always agree. My husband's lack of consideration is matched by his complete lack of spite. He is a man,' she sighed, 'of very good taste, which for me has always been a form of torture, because I am a good student and have been unable to prevent myself from learning his taste very thoroughly, to the extent that I have come to know

143

what he wants before he even wants it himself, and in the matter of women I have become positively prophetic, almost to the extent that I see them with his eyes and feel his own desire for them. So I learned in the end to close my eyes; and if only I had remembered to close my ears too, that morning in the kitchen, I might still be looking down at my plate to find that the nicest and most delicious morsel had somehow vanished.

'Today, when I took the glass lift up to his office, which is on the thirteenth floor, I emerged to see that everything there had changed. A complete re-decoration had occurred: the new theme was white, and being a man of extremes my husband had evidently decided that everything not white – including some of the people – had to be removed. And so Martha, my dear friend, his secretary, was no longer to be found in her place by the big window, at her old desk where she kept her packed lunch and her photographs of her children and a pair of flat shoes for walking, where we used to sit and talk and she would tell me all the things I needed to know and none of the things I didn't – Martha was gone, though my husband assured me that she had not been actually eradicated, merely given a big office of her own at the back, where she wouldn't be seen by visitors. In her place by the window, in the all-white world that

144

reminded me of nothing so much as that morning in the kitchen and the slice of fresh white goat's cheese I had to leave behind forever on its plate, sat a new girl. She, of course, wore white, and had skin pale as an albino's; and her hair, too, was entirely white, except for one long strand which came out like a plume from her head and was dyed – the only piece of colour in the place – the brightest blue. In the lift on the way down I marvelled at the sheer genius of the man, who had also managed, while I was there, to exact my forgiveness as stealthily as a pickpocket removes your wallet, and was returning me to the street lighter, though poorer, with that quill of blue perched in my thoughts like a feather in a beggar's cap.'

Marielle fell silent, her ridged face lifted, her enormous glittering eyes gazing straight ahead. It was quite common, the man to her left presently observed, for young people now to use their appearance as a means of shocking or disturbing others: he himself – and he was sure the same was true for all of us – had seen hairstyles far more extreme than the one Marielle described, not to mention tattoos and piercings of sometimes an apparently violent nature, which all the same said nothing whatever about their owners, who were often people of the greatest sweetness and docility. It had taken him a long time to accept this fact, for he was predisposed to be judgemental and to find the meaning of a thing commensurate with its appearance, and also to be frightened of what he didn't understand; and though he didn't, strictly speaking, comprehend the reasons why people might choose to mutilate themselves, he had learned not to read too much into it. If anything, he saw such outward extremes as the symbols of a correspondingly great inner emptiness, a futility that he believed came from the lack of engagement with any meaningful system of belief. His peers – and he was only twenty-four, though he was aware he looked somewhat older – were for the most part quite astonishingly indifferent to the religious and political debates of our times. But for him, political awakening had been the awakening of his whole sensibility, had given him a way of existing in the world, something about which he felt pride but also a certain anxiety, almost a kind of guilt, which he found difficult to explain.

This morning, for instance, on his way here he had walked through the part of the city where last summer – as everyone would recall – there were demonstrations, in which he and his political friends had proudly participated. He found himself following the exact route they had followed that day, treading streets he had not visited again until now, and found himself filled with emotion at the memories they brought back to him. Then, at a certain point, he passed through an alleyway on both sides of which the buildings were burnt-out shells: he could see through the glassless windows into the cavernous, ruined interiors, all blackened and ghostly and still filled with the mess and detritus of their own destruction, for in the whole year that had passed no one had come to clear it away. Quite how these buildings had been set alight he did not recall, but it had been towards evening, and the fires had been seen from all over Athens. News agencies had broadcast footage of the smoke billowing across the city that had been relayed all over the world; it was, he could not deny, part of the excitement of that night, as well as a necessary means – he believed – of getting the demonstrators' message across. Yet all he could feel, looking through into the desolate ruins, was shame, to the extent that he actually thought he heard his mother's voice, asking him whether it was really he that was responsible for all that mess, because people had told her so and until he confirmed it she wouldn't know whether or not to believe them.

As a child, he continued – his name, according to my drawing, was Christos – he had been extremely shy and awkward, to the point where his mother had decided to enrol him in dancing classes as a way of building his confidence. These classes, which took place in a nearby hall and were attended by local girls and a smaller number of local boys – barbarians all – were a torment to him on a scale that even now is difficult for him to convey. It was not only that he was overweight and physically unconfident: it was that he had a fear of exposure that drove him inexplicably, in such situations, to make himself fall over. It was a kind of vertigo, he said, such as drives people who are frightened of heights to want to jump; he simply couldn't bear being looked at, and to ask him to dance was like asking him to walk a high wire, where the thought of falling must be so ever-present that it would eventually bring itself about. And fall he did, repeatedly and with anguish, flailing humiliated among the twirling feet of the other children like a beached whale, and consequently subject to much mockery, until the dancing teacher was forced to suggest that he stop attending classes and he was allowed to stay at home.

'Imagine, then, my horror,' he said, 'when I finally went to university and fell in with a group of fine, committed, like-minded individuals such as I had dreamed my whole life of having as friends, only to discover that the chief hobby and pastime of this group, their greatest love – after politics – was dancing. Night after night they would invite me to dances and I would, of course, refuse. My closest associate in this social world, Maria, a girl with whom I had the most passionate political discussions, a girl I shared everything with, even my love of crosswords, of which we would complete several together each day – even Maria was disappointed in my refusal to participate in this traumatic activity. Trust me, she said, just as my mother had said before her – trust me, you'll enjoy it. I came to believe, in the end, that if I didn't dance I would lose Maria's friendship, while at the same time being certain that once she saw me dancing I would lose it anyway. There was no way out, and so I agreed one evening to accompany them to the club they always went to. It was not at all what I expected, for the reason that it had nothing to do with the modern world. It was a place devoted to the style and music of the nineteen-fifties: people came there dressed, as it were, in costume, and danced something called Lindy Hop. Seeing this, I was more terrified than ever; but perhaps,' he said, 'the best way to confront our fears is to put them in costume, so to speak; to translate them, for the simple act of translation very often renders things harmless. The habits – one might almost say the constraints – of one's personality and cast of mind are slipped free of; I found myself walking on to the dance floor,' Christos said, 'hand in hand with Maria, convinced that I should fall, and yet when the music started – an irresistible, happy music which, to this day, I am unable to hear without every trace of melancholy and doubt evaporating – I found myself not falling but flying, flying up and up, around and around, so fast and so high that I seemed to fly clear even of my body itself.'

My phone rang on the table in front of me. It was my younger son's number. I picked it up and said that I would call him back later.

'I'm lost,' he said. 'I don't know where I am.'

Holding the phone to my chest I told the group that there was a minor emergency and that we would take a short break. I went out and stood in the corridor, where there were noticeboards with lists and advertisements and bulletins pinned to them: apartments to rent, photocopying services, concerts forthcoming. I asked my son whether he could see a sign with a road name on it.

'I'll just look,' he said.

I could hear traffic in the background and the sound of his breathing. After a while he gave me the name of the street, and I asked him what on earth he was doing there.

'I'm trying to get to school,' he said.

I asked why he wasn't going to school the way I had arranged for him this week, with his friend Mark and Mark's mother.

'Mark isn't coming to school today,' he said. 'He's ill.'

I told him to turn around and walk back the way he had come, telling me the name of each street he passed, and when he reached the right one I told him to turn down it and carry straight on. After a few minutes, during which I listened to his puffing breath and the tapping of his feet on the pavement, he said: 'I can see it, I can see the building, it's all right, I can see the building.'

You're not late, I said, looking at my watch and calculating the time in England; you've got a few minutes to get your breath back. I reminded him of the directions in reverse that he was to follow afterwards and said I hoped he'd have a nice day.

'Thanks,' he said.

In the classroom the group was waiting, just as I had left it except that one student, a very large and soft-looking young girl who wore glasses with thick black frames, was eating an enormous savoury pastry whose meaty smell was quite overpowering. She held the bottom of the pastry in its paper bag while she bit slowly from the top, to prevent crumbs from falling. Beside her sat a young man as slim and dark and compact as she was soft and formless. He put up his hand fleetingly and withdrew it again. On his way here, he said, in a quiet, precise voice –

151

I looked down to find his name, which was Aris – on his way here he had passed, lying by the side of the road, the putrefying body of a dog, grotesquely swollen and cloaked in swarms of black flies. He had heard the sound of the flies from some way off, he added, and had wondered what it was. It was a sound that was menacing while also being curiously beautiful, so long as you couldn't see its source. He did not come from Athens, he continued, but his brother lives here and offered him a place to stay for the week. It was a very small apartment; he was sleeping on the sofa, in a room that was also the kitchen. He slept with his head right next to the fridge, on whose door there were various magnets he had had no choice but to examine, including one made of plastic in the shape of a pair of naked breasts, so crudely formed that the nipple on the right breast was significantly off-centre, a dissonance he had considered for many hours while lying there. His brother washed his clothes in the kitchen sink and then hung them all around the room to dry: he worked in an office and needed clean shirts every day. Every available chair in the room, as well as the shelves and window ledges, had a shirt draped over it. While drying, the shirts had taken the impress of the forms beneath them. Lying on the sofa, he had noticed this.

152

The girl beside him had by now finished her pastry and was occupied in folding the bag into a neat square, smoothing out the creases with her fingers. When she looked up she caught my eye and immediately dropped the paper square on to the table in front of her with a guilty expression. Her name was Rosa, she said, and she wasn't sure whether her own contribution would be permitted. She didn't know whether she had understood the exercise correctly. In any case, hers wasn't like the others, and it probably wouldn't count, but it was all she could think of. She hadn't really seen anything on her way here: all that had happened was that she had passed the park where her grandmother used to take her in the afternoons when she was smaller. There was a little playground there, with a swing she used to sit on while her grandmother pushed her. This morning she had seen the playground as she passed, and had seen the swing, and had remembered her grandmother and the pleasant afternoons they spent together. She fell silent. I thanked her, and she gazed at me mildly through her black-rimmed glasses.

The hour was nearly up. The woman sitting directly opposite me, whose somewhat startled face was positioned beneath the face of the clock on the wall, so that the two shapes had become joined or connected in my perception to the extent that I had almost forgotten she was there, now said that it had been interesting for her to realise how little she noticed of the objective world. Her consciousness, at this point – she was forty-three years old – was so crammed full not just of her own memories, obligations, dreams, knowledge and the plethora of her day-to-day responsibilities, but also of other people's – gleaned over years of listening, talking, empathising, worrying – that she was frightened most of all of the boundaries separating these numerous types of mental freight, the distinctions between them, crumbling away until she was no longer certain what had happened to her and what to other people she knew, or sometimes even what was or was not real. This morning, for instance, her sister had called her very early – neither of them sleeps very well, so they often talk at this hour – to tell her of the evening she and her husband had spent at a friend's house, where they were invited for dinner. The friend had just had her kitchen completely extended and refurbished, and the centrepiece was an enormous sunken glass panel in the ceiling that made the room as light and airy as a cathedral.

'My sister', she said, 'complimented her friend on this stunning effect, and the friend admitted that in fact she had borrowed the idea from another friend, who had had her kitchen refurbished some months

154

before. Since then, however, a most terrible thing had happened. The friend's friend had invited a large number of guests to dinner. Shortly before their arrival she had noticed a tiny crack in the glass of the panel, as though something small but sharp had fallen on it from above. She was annoyed, because the panel had cost a considerable amount of money, and being all of one piece she didn't see any alternative but to replace the whole thing, despite the fact that only one small area had been affected. The guests arrived, and during the course of the evening an incredible storm came in over Athens. The rain came down in torrents as the group sat and ate beneath the glass panel. They were marvelling at the acoustic and visual effect of the water on the glass when, with a great groaning and creaking, the whole thing suddenly collapsed on top of them, the flaw in the glass apparently having weakened the structure to the point where it could not bear the weight of the water falling on it.'

The woman paused. 'This,' she said, 'you will recall, was told to me by my sister over the telephone, a story that neither affected her nor, strictly speaking, concerned her. And since no one, amazingly, was hurt, it wasn't a story that would shock people and that you would tell for that reason. Nor did it really affect the friend who had told it to her in the first place, except by association, because she had a panel in her ceiling of the same type. So I received it, as it were, third-hand, but it is as real to me as if I had experienced it myself. All morning I was troubled by it. Yet like most people I hear of terrible occurrences – nearly all of them far worse – every day, through the newspapers and the television, and I wondered why this one had taken a place in my mind among my own memories and experiences, so that I was having difficulty telling them apart. The reality of my life is largely concerned with what are called middle-class values – the people that I know refurbish their houses often, as I do myself, and they invite other people to these houses for dinner. But there is a difference, because the people in the story sound a little grander than the people I know, most of whom could not afford to put a glass panel in the ceiling, though they would very much like to. My sister, however, moves in slightly more exalted circles than I do: this is something I am aware of as a source of tension in our relationship. I am, I admit, slightly jealous of her social life and of the kinds of people she meets, and sometimes I think she could do more to include me in the more interesting world she inhabits.

'The second reason,' she continued, 'has to do with the story itself, and with the tiny flaw in the glass panel that eventually led to its entire collapse under pressure: the actual pressure of the water, and the more mysterious and intangible pressure of the people beneath it, who were admiring it while assuming absolutely that it would hold. When it did not, it became the cause of unutterable damage and destruction, almost an instrument of evil, and the symbolism of this arrangement of facts has a certain significance for me.' She was silent for a while, the juddering second hand moving around the clock face above her head. I looked at my chart and found that her name was Penelope. 'I would like', she resumed, 'to see the world more innocently again, more impersonally, but I have no idea how to achieve this, other than by going somewhere completely unknown, where I have no identity and no associations. But how such a thing could be accomplished, and even where such a place might be, I have no idea; not to mention the relationships and responsibilities themselves,' she concluded, 'which drive me mad but at the same time make escape from them impossible.'

Each member of the group had now spoken, except for one, a woman whose name on my chart was Cassandra and whose expression I had watched grow sourer and sourer as the hour passed, who had made her displeasure known by a series of increasingly indiscreet groans and sighs, and who now sat with her arms implacably folded, shaking her head. I asked

157

her whether she had anything, before we concluded, to contribute, and she said that she did not. She had obviously been mistaken, she said: she had been told this was a class about learning to write, something that as far as she was aware involved using your imagination. She didn't know what I thought had been achieved here, and she wasn't all that interested in finding out. At least Ryan, she said, had taught them something. She would be asking the organisers to refund her money, and would make damn sure they got her feedback. I don't know who you are, she said to me, getting to her feet and collecting her things, but I'll tell you one thing, you're a lousy teacher.

# VII

My neighbour asked whether I'd had time to do any sightseeing yet. We were in the car again, on the rackety road to the marina, with the windows down and his shirtsleeves flapping madly in the breeze.

I said that I had visited Athens several times before, and was familiar with the sights, though that did not altogether explain why I had as yet felt no urge to seek them out. He was surprised: he hadn't realised I'd been here so often. He himself went to London, for example, all the time, but for some reason it hadn't occurred to him that the same principle could work in reverse. When was the last time I had come? Three years ago, I said. He was silent for a while, his small eyes narrowed with a faraway look on the horizon.

'Three years ago,' he said musingly. 'At that time, I had just moved back to Athens myself.'

I asked where he had gone to, and why, and he said that he had spent a period living and working in London. He had been offered a very good job by a bank there, he continued, and though he didn't particularly want to give up the freedom of his life here, and especially his boat, he had a sense it might be the last such offer that came his way. And Athens at the time seemed full of his failures, or at least of things that had come to an end and in which he could find no possibility of renewal. In fact, he felt quite surprised, he said, to have been offered this job, because his opinion of himself had become very low. That is always a dangerous moment, he said, to make a big decision, when you are not sure of what you deserve. Evidently his friends shared his opinion, because all of them urged him, without hesitation, to take it. It is interesting how keen people are for you to do something they would never dream of doing themselves, how enthusiastically they drive you to your own destruction: even the kindest ones, the ones that are most loving, can rarely have your interests truly at heart, because usually they are advising you from within lives of greater security and greater confinement, where escape is not a reality but simply something they dream of sometimes. Perhaps, he said, we are all like animals in the zoo, and once we see that one of us has got out of the enclosure we shout at him to run like mad, even though it will only result in him becoming lost.

I said his image reminded me of a scene from an opera I liked – in fact I had found a recording of it in Clelia's apartment – called *The Cunning Little Vixen*, in which a fox is caught by a hunter and kept in a farmyard with the other animals. He keeps her because he loves her, despite the fact she is destructive, and there is a value for her too in his attention, though its consequence is her captivity. But her nature drives her to seek the wild, and one day she escapes the farmyard and finds her way back into the forest; but instead of feeling liberated she is terrified, for having lived in the farmyard most of her life she has forgotten how to be free. He was not familiar with that opera, my neighbour said; he, however, approached the prospect of the job in London with a reverse kind of fatalism, as though the very freedom of his life was something for which he was at last going to pay by going into harness. He, the scion of playboys and millionaires, would finally observe the penal servitude of a nine-to-five: he sold his house in Athens, bought a small flat in an upmarket part of the English capital, and took the boat out of the water. It is the only time, he said, in the twenty-five years of its history that the boat has left the element in which it lives. He had made arrangements for it to be stored in a warehouse in the centre of Athens; it is difficult, even now, for him to convey the emotion he felt watching it be lifted out of the sea and placed on a flatbed truck, which he drove behind all the way in his car, and then interred in its container deep in the city. And then off he went to London, sensing that he himself was about to suffer much the same fate.

I asked him what it was that brought him back from that interment, and he smiled. A phone call, he said. It was his second winter in London, and he was sunk in a dreary and lonely existence, trudging through the rain to work and back again, putting in eighteen-hour days at the bank and eating takeaways late at night in his carpeted prison, when the owner of the warehouse in Athens called him to say that there had been a break-in and that the boat's engine had been stolen. The next day he handed in his resignation and was on a flight back. How refreshing it was, he said, how affirming, to feel such certainty. He had come almost to believe he was a person with no clear feelings about anything, particularly since the history of his loves had led him into such swamplands of failure, yet this attack on his property returned him to joy and life as though he had won the lottery. For the first time in years he knew what he wanted. The first thing he did, on his return, was buy the best engine he could find, though it did, he accepted, have a little more power than he needed.

We were by now approaching the marina, and he asked whether I wouldn't like to stop for some coffee or a drink before we set sail. There was no need to hurry, after all; we had all the time in the world. He seemed to remember hearing there was a new place that had just opened, somewhere along the beach; he took his foot off the accelerator and dawdled, peering through the windscreen at the dusty roadside and its string of bars and restaurants, beyond which lay the sand and the water with its frill of surf. Abruptly he steered off into the dirt at the side of the verge and stopped, outside a place with palm trees in white cubic planters and a terrace open to the sea with arrangements of white cubic furniture. There was the sound of jazz, and waiters dressed in black were gliding around the empty furniture, in the shade of an asymmetric white canopy like a giant sail. He asked me if this was all right. I said it looked very impressive, and we got out of the car and went and sat at a table, beside one of the palm trees.

It was important, my neighbour said, to remember to enjoy yourself along the way: in a sense, this had become his philosophy of life these days. His third wife, he said, had been so puritanical that he sometimes felt no amount of pit-stops and pauses would make up for the years he spent with her, in which every event was faced head-on, unanaesthetised, and every little pleasure interrogated and either deemed unnecessary or else written down – with tax added on, he said – in a notebook she kept with her at all times for the purpose. Never had he met someone who was so unmediatedly the product of their family, a Calvinist household obsessed with thrift and the avoidance of waste, though she did, he said, have one weakness, for Formula One racing, which she would sometimes indulge by watching on television, being particularly riveted by the scenes of the winner spraying the cheering crowd with wasted champagne. He had met her at a time when his finances had been devastated by his second divorce, and so her song of parsimony had been, briefly, music to his ears. At the wedding, asked by friends what it was she saw in him – a pertinent enough question, he conceded, at the time – she had replied, I find him interesting.

He ordered two coffees from one of the circling waiters, and for a while we watched the people on the beach from our shady seclusion, their bare bodies smudged by the haze of heat, so that they looked somehow primordial, lying or moving slowly, half naked, along the shore. I said that it didn't sound such a bad reason to marry someone, and he looked somewhat darkly out to sea. She knew nothing whatever of the physical side of life, he said, despite the fact that she was nearly forty when they met. Her purity and simplicity attracted him, after the knowing seductiveness of his second wife, but in fact she was a woman

164

entirely without romance, entirely without sex, and the nun-like existence she had led previously – and as far as he knew, had resumed when they parted – was not the consequence of a lack of opportunity but was the accurate reflection of her nature. The intimate side of their marriage was an unmitigated disaster, for once they had conceived a child, which they did almost straight away, she simply could not understand why there was any further need for them to have relations. It was a blow for him, and one he tried hard to forestall, but one night she asked him very frankly how many more times she ought to expect that he would require her to participate in an act she evidently found unenjoyable as well as incomprehensible, and after that he lost heart.

Yet he did concede, he said, that through this woman he had had his first and only glimpse of a different kind of relationship, indeed a different kind of life, one that was based on principles he had never paid any heed to: decency, equality, virtue, honour, self-sacrifice, as well as thrift of course. She had a great deal of common sense, and an infallible grasp of discipline and routine and household management, and he found both his finances and his health in better order than they had been for years. Theirs was a calm and well-run home, with predictability – something he had always actively avoided, something he had, one could almost say, feared – as its cherished principle. She reminded him of his mother, and in fact it transpired that that was what she expected him to call her, 'mother', while she likewise would address him as 'father', for it was how her parents had always addressed one another and was all she knew. That was obviously, for him, another nail in the coffin, but all the same he had to admit that she was never exploitative, or silly, or selfish: she was and remains an excellent mother to their son, who is the only one of his children – he had again to admit – that he could call stable and well-adjusted. She did not attempt to destroy him in the divorce proceedings, but instead accepted her share of responsibility for what had happened, so that together they could work out the best way to arrange things, for themselves and their child. I realised, he said, that my whole understanding of life had been, in some sense, profoundly adversarial: the story of men and women, for me, was ultimately a story of war, to the extent that I wondered sometimes whether I had an actual horror of peace, whether I sought to stir things up out of a fear of boredom that was also, you might say, a fear of death itself. I said to you, when we first met, that I regard love – the love between man and woman – as the great regenerator of happiness, but it is also the regenerator of interest. It is what you perhaps would call the storyline – he smiled – and so, he said, for all the virtues of my third wife, I discovered that a life with no story was not, in the end, a life that I could live.

He paid the bill, waving away my offers of money after a brief but observable hesitation, and we stood to leave. In the car he asked how my class that morning had gone, and I found myself telling him about the woman who had attacked me, about my sense – all through the hour – of her growing resentment and anger and my increasingly certain knowledge that at some point she would strike. He listened, sombrely, as I relayed the details of her tirade, the worst aspect of which, I said, was its element of impersonality, which had caused me to feel like nothing, a non-entity, even while she was giving me, so to speak, her full attention. This feeling, of being negated at the same time as I was exposed, had had a particularly powerful effect on me, I said. It had seemed to encapsulate something that didn't, strictly speaking, exist. He was silent for a while as we drove to the marina. He stopped the car and switched off the engine.

'I was at home this morning,' he said, 'at home in my kitchen, making myself a glass of orange juice, and I suddenly had the very strong feeling that something bad was happening to you.' He stared through the windscreen at the glittering water, where the white boats were moving up and down. 'I find it quite extraordinary,' he said, 'this very clear signal that I received. I even remember looking at my watch: it must have been at exactly that time that I sent you the message asking if you would like to come out on the boat again today. Am I correct?' I smiled and said that it was true, I had received his message at more or less exactly that moment. 'That is very unusual,' he said. 'A very strong connection.'

He got out of the car and I watched him make his way, with his slightly waddling walk, to the water's edge, where he bent down to pull out the dripping rope. We repeated the previous day's routine, me waiting while he made things ready on deck and then the courtly pas de deux whereby we changed places, the rope passing between our hands. When everything was done he started the engine and we chugged away from the mooring, from the heat of the jetty and the car park that looked like a field of brilliant metals in the dust, the sun flashing and glinting in the dark windows. We did not go so fast, this time, as the day before; whether through consideration or because, having demonstrated his power, my neighbour could now conserve his energies, I did not know. I sat on the padded bench, his naked back once more before my eyes, the wind scouring the

deck, and thought of the strange transitions from en-
chantment to disenchantment and back again that
moved through human affairs like cloudbanks, sometimes portentous and grey and sometimes mere distant inscrutable shapes that blotted out the sun for a
while and then just as carelessly revealed it again. My
neighbour called back to me, over the noise of the
engine, that we were just now passing the promon-
tory and temple of Sounion, from whose cliffs, in
Greek legend, the father of Theseus threw himself
when he saw his son's ship returning to land wearing
the black sail that conveyed, wrongly, the news of his
death. I looked and saw a ruined temple in the distance like a little broken diadem on the hilltop, just
before the land tumbled down to meet the sea.

Mixed messages, my neighbour continued, as we
approached the cove and started to slow down, were
a cruel plot device that did sometimes have their
counterpart in life: his own brother, the one who
had died a few years ago, a dear and generous person, suffered his fatal heart attack while waiting for
a friend to come to lunch. He had given the man
– who happened, moreover, to be a doctor – the
wrong address, for he had just moved into a new
apartment and hadn't yet memorised the full details,
and so while his friend was searching for him in a
street of a similar name on the other side of town,

he was lying on his kitchen floor with his life ebbing away, a life, what's more, that apparently could easily have been saved had he been reached in time. His older brother, the reclusive Swiss millionaire, had responded to these events by having a complex system of alarms installed in his own apartment, for though he was a man who would never forget his own address he was also entirely friendless and miserly and had never had a lunch guest in his life; and indeed when his own heart attack came – which their family medical history made a likelihood – he simply pressed the nearest emergency button and within minutes was in a helicopter, being whisked to a top cardiac unit in Geneva. Sometimes it was as well, he said – and he was thinking of Theseus's father here – not to take no for an answer, almost as a point of principle.

I said that, on the contrary, I had come to believe more and more in the virtues of passivity, and of living a life as unmarked by self-will as possible. One could make almost anything happen, if one tried hard enough, but the trying – it seemed to me – was almost always a sign that one was crossing the currents, was forcing events in a direction they did not naturally want to go, and though you might argue that nothing could ever be accomplished without going against nature to some extent, the artificiality of that vision and its consequences had become – to put it bluntly – anathema to me. There was a great difference, I said, between the things I wanted and the things that I could apparently have, and until I had finally and forever made my peace with that fact, I had decided to want nothing at all.

My neighbour was silent for a considerable length of time. He steered the boat into the deserted cove, where the seabirds stood on the rocks and the water whirled in its little inlet, and took the anchor out of its compartment. He leaned over me to cast it over the side, and slowly paid out the chain until he felt it resting on the bottom.

'Has there really been no one?' he asked.

There had, I said, been someone. We were still very good friends. But I hadn't wanted to carry on with it. I was trying to find a different way of living in the world.

Now that we had come to a stop, the heat had intensified. The sun shone directly on the padded bench where I sat, and the only patch of shade was directly beneath the canopy, where my neighbour stood with his arms folded, leaning against the side of the boat. It would have been awkward to go and stand there with him. I could feel the skin on my back burning. Just then he moved, but it was only to re-place the lid of the compartment where he kept the anchor, and he returned to his original position. He understood, he said, that I was still in a great deal of pain. Being with me had reminded him of episodes in his own life he had not thought of for many years, and was causing him to revisit some of these feelings himself. His first marriage, he said, had really come to an end on a day when they had had a large family party, a lunch to which all the relatives on both sides had been invited and which they held at their home in the suburbs of Athens, a house big enough and grand enough to accommodate everyone. The party had been a success, everything had been eaten and drunk and cleared away and the guests had finally departed, and my neighbour, exhausted, had lain down on the sofa to take a nap. His wife was in the kitchen doing the last of the dishes, the children were out playing somewhere, there was a cricket match making its slow progress on the television, and amidst this scene of domestic contentment my neighbour fell into a profound sleep.

For a moment he was silent, leaning against the side of the boat, his fleshy white-haired arms with their ropes of veins folded across his chest.

'I believe,' he resumed presently, 'that what my wife did then was premeditated, that she saw me lying there and intended to force a confession from me by surprise. She came to the sofa and shook

drawn not so much to this specific woman as to the concept of excitement itself, a prospect that seemed – as he had said, from far away – to welcome him with its largeness and brightness, to offer him an anonymity that might also constitute a re-evaluation of his whole persona, he who was known so thoroughly and yet so limitingly by his wife and before that by his parents, his siblings, his uncles and aunts. It was to be free of their knowledge of him that he sought that brighter world, which admittedly, in his youth, he had made the mistake of believing to be far more extensive than it actually was. He has been disillusioned more times than he could count in his relationships with women. Yet part of that feeling – the feeling of excitement that is also a rebirth of identity – has attended all his experiences of falling in love; and in the end, despite everything that has happened, these have been the most compelling moments of his life.

I said I wondered how he could fail to see the relationship between disillusionment and knowledge in what he had told me. If he could only love what he did not know, and be loved in return on that same basis, then knowledge became an inexorable disenchantment, for which the only cure was to fall in love with someone new. There was a silence. He stood there, looking all at once grizzled and old, his hairy arms folded above his paunch, his swimming trunks

175

sagging between his legs, his birdlike face almost fossilised into its quizzical expression. The silence extended itself, there amid the glittering water and the glaring sun. I became aware of the sound of the water sucking at the sides of the boat, of the harsh cries of the seagulls on their rocks, of the faint sound of engines coming from the mainland. My neighbour lifted his head and looked out to sea, his chin raised, his eyes searching the horizon. There was a certain stiffness in his manner, a self-consciousness, like that of an actor about to deliver a too-famous line.

'I have been asking myself', he said, 'why it is that I find myself so attracted to you.'

He spoke so momentously that I couldn't help laughing out loud. He looked surprised and some-what confused by this, but all the same he came to-wards me, out of the shade and into the sun, heavily yet inexorably, like a prehistoric creature issuing from its cave. He bent down, moving awkwardly around the coldbox at my feet, and tried to embrace me from the side, putting one arm around my shoulders while attempting to bring his face into contact with mine. I could smell his breath, and feel his bushy grey eye-brows grazing my skin. The great beak of his nose loomed at the edge of my field of vision, his claw-like hands with their white fur fumbled at my shoulders; I felt myself, momentarily, being wrapped around in his greyness and dryness, as though the prehistoric creature were wrapping me in its dry bat-like wings, felt his scaly mouth miss its mark and move blindly at my cheek. Through the whole thing I stayed rigidly still, staring straight ahead of me at the steering wheel, until at last he withdrew, back into the shade.

I said that I needed to get out of the sun and was going into the water, and he nodded wordlessly, watching me. I jumped over the side and swam out across the cove, remembering the family on the boat that had been here the last time, and feeling a strange ache almost of homesickness for them, which became a feeling of longing for my own children, who suddenly seemed so far away that it was hard to believe they even existed. I swam for as long as I could, but in the end I returned to the boat and slowly climbed the ladder. My neighbour was occupied with some task, untying and adjusting the narrow ropes to which the buoys were attached that ran along the sides. I stood on the deck, dripping, and watched him, a towel wrapped around my shoulders where my skin hurt from the sun. He had a penknife in his hand, a large red Swiss Army knife with a long ridged blade, and was cutting the frayed ends off the ropes with a sense of purpose, his thick upper arms bulging as he sawed. He retied the ropes while I watched, and then strolled along the deck towards me, the knife still in his hand. Had I had a nice swim, he asked.

Yes, I said. Thank you, I said, for taking the trouble to bring me somewhere so lovely. But he had to understand, I said, that I was not interested in a relationship with any man, not now and probably not ever again. The sun beat uncomfortably on my face while I was speaking. What I valued most of all was friendship, I said, while he played with the knife in his hand, snapping the different blades in and out. I watched pieces of steel appear and disappear in his fingers, each one so distinctly shaped, some of them long and narrow and piercing, others strangely spiked and horned. And now, I said, if he didn't mind, we probably ought to be going back.

Slowly he inclined his head. Of course, he said; he also had things he needed to do. Perhaps I could wait until he just cooled off himself and then we would be on our way. While he was swimming, straight out in a furrow in his heavy, short-lived crawl, his phone rang somewhere on the deck. I sat there in the sun while it rang and rang, waiting for it to stop.

# VIII

My friend Elena was very beautiful: Ryan was beside himself. He'd been ambling along the street and spied us sitting at a bar. She's in a different league, he said, when she excused herself to go and make a phone call. Elena was thirty-six, intelligent, exquisitely dressed. She's another proposition entirely, he said.

The bar was on a narrow side street so steep that the chairs and tables slanted and wobbled on the uneven pavement. I had just watched a woman, a tourist, fall backwards into a planter, her shopping bags and guidebooks flying out to all sides of her, while her husband sat startled in his chair, apparently more embarrassed than concerned. He wore a pair of binoculars around his neck, and hiking boots on his feet that remained punctiliously tucked beneath the table while his wife flailed in the dry, spiky greenery. Eventually he put out an arm across the table to help her back up, but it was beyond her reach and so she was forced to struggle out on her own.

179

I asked Ryan what he had done today, and he said that he had gone to a museum or two, and then spent the afternoon wandering around the Agora, though to be honest he was a bit the worse for wear. He'd had a late night with some of the younger students, he said. They'd taken him to a series of bars, each one a good forty minutes' walk from the next. I was feeling my age, he said. I just wanted a drink – I didn't much care where I got it or how it came, and I certainly didn't need to walk to the other side of town to drink it off a lip-shaped sofa. But they're a nice enough crowd, he said. They'd been teaching him a few words of Greek – he wasn't sure how much change he'd get for them, his pronunciation being what it was, but all the same it was interesting to get a sense of things on the verbal level. He hadn't realised how many English meanings came from Greek compounds. For instance the word *ellipsis*, he'd been told, could literally be translated as 'to hide behind silence'. It's fascinating stuff, he said.

Elena came back and sat down again. Her appearance, this evening, was particularly Lorelei-like. She seemed to be composed entirely of curves and waves.

'My friend will meet us shortly,' she said, 'in a place not far from here.'

Ryan lifted an eyebrow.

'You two off somewhere?'

'We're meeting Melete,' Elena said. 'You are familiar with the name? She is one of the pre-eminent lesbian poets of Greece.'

Ryan said that actually he was peaked; he might have to leave us to it. He'd had a late night, as he'd said. And then he'd come back to the apartment at three in the morning to find great winged scarab-like creatures flying all around the place and had had to bash them all to death with his shoe. Someone – it wasn't him – had left a light on and a window open. All the same, it had struck him how little he cared about cheerfully massacring the bastards: when he was younger, he would have been too frightened. You become brave just by being a parent, he said. Or maybe it's just you become disinhibited. He'd felt this last night, socialising with people in their twenties. He'd forgotten how physically shy they were.

The quick hot dusk was falling, and soon the narrow street had filled up with darkness. The man in the hiking boots and his wife had gone. Ryan's phone rang and he picked it up, showing us the photograph of a grinning, toothless child that was pulsing on the screen. Must be bedtime, he said; I'll be seeing you folks. He stood and with a wave of his hand walked away down the hill, talking. Elena paid the bill with her credit card from the office – she was an editor at a publishing house and so strictly speaking, she said, we could consider our meeting to be work – and we walked up towards the light and noise of the main street. She trod beside me with quick, light steps in her high-heeled sandals; her dress was a shift of a knitted material the same dark gold colour as her long waving hair. All the men we passed looked at her, one after the other. We crossed Kolonaki Square, which was empty now except for one or two dark figures lying huddled on the benches. A woman sat on one of the low concrete walls, her legs strangely spattered with dried mud, eating crackers from a packet. A little boy stood near her at the kiosk, looking at the chocolate bars. We walked up an alleyway and came out in a crowded little square filled with the noise of people packed into the restaurant terraces all around its four sides, their faces in the darkness garish with electric light. The heat and the noise and electric light in the darkness produced an atmosphere of unvarying excitement, like a wave continually breaking, and though the restaurants looked indistinguishable from one another, Elena passed several before stopping very decidedly at one. This was the place, she said; Melete had said we should get a table and wait for her here. She wove her way through the tables and spoke to a waiter, who stood there implacable as a policeman and began shaking his head while she talked.

'He says they are full,' she said, crestfallen, her arms dropping to her sides.

Her disappointment was so intense that she didn't move, but stayed standing among the tables and staring at them as though willing them to yield to her. The waiter, observing this performance, appeared to change his mind: there was, he decided, room, if we were happy to sit – Elena translated – over in that corner. He showed us to the table, which Elena scrutinised as though she might not take it after all. It is a bit too close to the wall, she said to me. Do you think we will be all right here? I said I didn't mind sitting next to the wall: she could sit in the place further out if she preferred.

'Why do you wear these dark clothes?' she said to me, once we had sat down. 'I don't understand it. I wear light things when it is hot. Also you look a little sunburned,' she added. 'Between your shoulders, just there, the skin is burned.'

I told her I had spent the afternoon on a boat, with someone I didn't know well enough to ask to put sun cream on my back. She asked who this person was. Was it a man?

Yes, I said, a man I had met on the airplane and had got talking to. Elena's eyes widened with surprise.

'I would not have thought it likely', she said, 'that

you would go off on a boat with a complete stranger. What is he like? Do you like him?'

I closed my eyes and tried to summon up my feelings for my neighbour. When I opened them again Elena was still looking at me, waiting. I said that I had become so unused to thinking about things in terms of whether I liked them or whether I didn't that I couldn't answer her question. My neighbour was merely a perfectly good example of something about which I could only feel absolute ambivalence.

'But you still let him take you out on his boat,' she said.

It was hot, I said. And the terms on which we had left the harbour were strictly – or so I thought – the terms of friendship. I described his attempt to kiss me, when we were anchored far out to sea. I said that he was old, and that though it would be cruel to call him ugly, I had found his physical advances as repellent as they were surprising. It had never occurred to me that he would do such a thing; or more accurately, before she pointed out that I would have to be an imbecile not to have seen it as a possibility, I thought he wouldn't dare do such a thing. I had thought the differences between us were obvious, but to him they weren't.

She hoped, Elena said, that I had made that fact clear to him. I said that, on the contrary, I had come up with all manner of excuses to spare his feelings. She was silent for a while.

'If,' she said presently, 'you had told him the truth, if you had said to him, look, you are old and short and fat, and though I like you the only reason I am really here is to get a ride on your boat –' she began to laugh, fanning her face with the menu '– if you had said those things to him, you understand, you would have heard some truths in return. If you had been frank you would have elicited frankness.'

She herself, she said, had visited the very depths of disillusionment in the male character by being honest in precisely this way: men who had claimed one minute to be dying of love for her were openly insulting her the next, and it was only, in a sense, when she had reached this place of mutual frankness that she could work out who she herself was and what she actually wanted. What she couldn't stand, she said, was pretence of any kind, especially the pretence of desire, wherein someone feigned the need to possess her wholly when in fact what he wanted was to use her temporarily. She herself, she said, was quite willing to use others too, but she only recognised it once they had admitted this intention in themselves.

Unseen by Elena, a slender woman with a fox-like face was approaching our table. I took this to be

185

Melete. She came stealthily behind Elena's chair and rested her hand on her shoulder.

'Yassas,' she said sombrely.

She wore a mannish black waistcoat and trousers, and her short straight hair fell in two glossy black wings on either side of her narrow, shy, pointed face.

Elena twisted around in her seat to greet her.

'You as well!' she exclaimed. 'These dark clothes, both of you – why do you always wear dark things?'

Melete took her time replying to this. She sat down in the vacant chair, sat back and crossed her legs, withdrew a packet of cigarettes from her waistcoat pocket and lit one.

'Elena,' she said, 'it is not polite to talk about how people look. It is our own business what we wear.' She reached across the table and shook my hand. 'It's noisy here tonight,' she said, looking around. 'I've just taken part in a poetry reading where the audience numbered six people. The contrast is quite noticeable.'

She picked up the wine list from the table and began to study it, the cigarette smoking in her fingers, her fine nose twitching slightly, her glossy hair falling forward over her cheeks.

One of the six, she added, glancing up, was a man who came to nearly every public appearance she gave, and would sit in the front row making faces at her. This had been happening for several years now. She would look up from her lectern, not just in Athens but in other cities that are quite far away, and there he would be right in front of her, sticking his tongue out and making rude signs.

'But do you know him?' Elena said, astonished. 'Have you ever spoken to him?'

'I taught him,' Melete said. 'He was an under-graduate student of mine, a long time ago, when I lectured at the university.'

'And what did you do to him? Why does he torment you in this way?'

'I have to assume', Melete said, puffing gravely on her cigarette, 'that he doesn't have a reason. I did nothing to him: I barely even remember teaching him. He passed through one of my classes, where there were more than fifty students. I didn't notice him. I've tried, obviously, to remember some particular incident but there isn't one. You could spend your whole life', she said, 'trying to trace events back to your own mistakes. People in legend thought that their misfortunes could be traced back to their failure to offer libations to certain gods. But there is another explanation,' she said, 'which is simply that he is mad.'

'Have you ever tried to talk to him?' Elena said.

Melete slowly shook her head.

'As I said, I barely remember him, though I don't forget people easily. So you could say that this attack has come from the place I least expected. In fact it would almost be true to say that this student was the very last person I had ever considered to pose a threat to me.'

At times, Melete continued, it had almost seemed to her that this fact was what had created his behaviour. Her sense of reality, in other words, had created an attack on itself, had created something outside itself that mocked and hated her. But as I say, she said, those thoughts belong to the world of religious sensibility, which has become in our times the language of neurosis.

'I prefer to call it madness,' she said, 'whether his or my own, and so instead I have tried to become fond of him. I look up and there he always is, waggling his fingers and sticking out his tongue. He is in fact entirely dependable, more faithful to me than any lover I've ever had. I try to love him back.'

She closed the wine list and put up her finger to summon the waiter. Elena said something to her in Greek and a brief dispute ensued, which the waiter joined halfway through and in which he appeared conclusively to take Melete's side, taking the order from her with much brusque nodding of his head despite Elena's continued petitions.

'Elena knows nothing about wine,' Melete said, to me.

Elena seemed to take no offence at this remark. She returned to the subject of Melete's persecutor.

'What you have described,' she said, 'is complete subjection. The idea that you should love your enemies is patently ridiculous. It is entirely a religious proposition. To say that you love what you hate and what hates you is the same as admitting you have been defeated, that you accept your oppression and are just trying to make yourself feel better about it. And saying you love him is the same as saying you don't want to know what he really thinks of you. If you talked to him,' she said, 'you would find out.'

I watched the people at the other tables and at the tables on the adjoining terraces, all packed so tightly that the whole square seemed to be aflame with conversation. Here and there beggars moved among the talking people, who often took some time to realise they were there, and then either gave them something or brushed them away. Several times I saw this repeated, the wraith-like figure standing unnoticed behind the chair of the person obliviously eating, talking, absorbed in life. A tiny, desiccated, hooded woman was moving among the tables close to us, and presently she approached ours, murmuring, the little claw of her hand outstretched. I watched Melete place some coins in her palm and say a few words to her, gently stroking her fingers.

'What he thinks is of no importance,' she continued. 'If I found out more about what he thinks, I might start to confuse him with myself. And I don't compose myself from other people's ideas, any more than I compose a verse from someone else's poem.'

'But to him this is a game, a fantasy,' Elena said. 'Men like to play this game. And they actually fear your honesty, because then the game is spoiled. By not being honest with a man you allow him to continue his game, to live in his fantasy.'

As if to prove her point, my phone sounded on the table. It was a text from my neighbour: *I miss you*, it said.

It was only when you got beyond people's fantasies, Elena continued, about themselves and one another, that you accessed a level of reality where things assumed their true value and were what they seemed to be. Some of those truths, admittedly enough, were ugly, but others were not. The worst thing, it seemed to her, was to be dealing with one version of a person when quite another version existed out of sight. If a man had a nasty side to his character, she wanted to get to it immediately and confront it. She didn't want it roaming unseen in the hinterland of the relationship: she wanted to provoke it, to draw it forth, lest it strike her when her back was turned.

Melete laughed. 'According to that logic,' she said, 'there can be no relationship at all. There can only be people stalking one another.'

The waiter brought the wine, a small unlabelled bottle the colour of ink, and Melete began to pour it out.

'It's true,' Elena said, 'that my own need for provocation is something other people seem to find very difficult to understand. Yet to me it has always made perfect sense. But I do admit that it has brought nearly all of my relationships to an end, because it is inevitable that that end is also – as you say, by the same logic – something I will feel driven to provoke. If the relationship is going to end, in other words, I want to know it and confront it as soon as possible. Sometimes,' she said, 'this process is so quick that the relationship is over almost as soon as it has begun. Very often I have felt that my relationships have had no story, and the reason is because I have jumped ahead of myself, the way I used to turn the pages of a book to find out what happens in the final chapter. I want to know everything straight away. I want to know the content without living through the time span.'

The person she was involved with now, she said – a man named Konstantin – had given her for the first time in her life a cause to fear these tendencies in herself, for the reason that – unlike, if she was to be honest, any other man of her experience – she judged him to be her equal. He was intelligent, handsome, amusing, an intellectual: she liked being beside him, liked the reflection of herself he gave her. And he was a man in possession of his own morality and attitudes, so that she felt – for the first time, as she had said – a kind of invisible boundary around him, a line it was clear, though no one ever said as much, she ought not to cross. That line, that boundary, was something she had never encountered so palpably in any other man, men whose defences were usually cobbled together out of fantasies and deceptions that no one – themselves least of all – would blame her for wanting to break through. And so not only did she feel a sense of prohibition around Konstantin, a sense that he would regard her raiding him for his truth much as he would have regarded her breaking into his house and stealing his things, she had actually become frightened of the very thing she loved him for, his equality with herself.

It remained, therefore, within his grasp, this weapon of which she had been so quick to disarm every other man: the power to hurt her. At a party recently, where she had taken Konstantin and introduced him to many of her friends, she had been enjoying the feeling of showing him off to her social circle, seeing his handsomeness and his wit and his integrity through their eyes – and vice versa, because this was a house of artists and other interesting people from her world – and she had started to eavesdrop a little on his conversation with a woman she knew but didn't like very much, a woman called Yanna. It was partly out of spite towards Yanna that she had given into the temptation to eavesdrop: she wanted to hear Konstantin speak, and to imagine Yanna's jealousy at the intelligence and good looks of Elena's boyfriend. Yanna was asking about Konstantin's children, of which he has two from a previous marriage, and then, quite casually, while Elena was listening, Yanna asked him whether he'd like to have any more children. No, he said, while Elena, listening, felt as though knives were being plunged into her from all sides; no, he didn't think he wanted any more children, he was happy with things as they were.

She raised her glass to her lips, her hand trembling.

'We had never,' she continued quietly, 'discussed the question of children, but it is obvious that for me it remains open, that I may very well want to have children. Suddenly this party I was enjoying, where I had felt so happy, became a torture. I was unable to laugh or smile or speak to anyone properly; I just wanted to go away and be alone, but I had to stay there with him until it was over. And of course he had noticed that I was upset, and kept asking me what was wrong; and for the whole of the rest of that evening and night he kept asking me to tell him what was wrong. In the morning he was due to go away on business for a few days. I had to tell him, he said. It was impossible for him to go to the airport and get on a plane with me in this upset state. But of course it would have been so humiliating to tell him, because I had overheard something not meant for my ears, and also because of the subject itself, which ought to have been approached so differently.

'It seemed to me that this was a situation it was impossible to get out of, while still thinking as well of one another as we had before. I had this feeling,' she continued, 'which I have had since and which gets worse each time we argue, that we were caught in a net of words, tangled up in all these strings and knots, and that each of us thought there was something we could say that would set us free, but the more words we spoke the more tangles and knots there were. I find myself thinking of the simplicity of the time before we had said one syllable to one another: that is the time I would like to go back to,' she said, 'the time just before we first opened our mouths to speak.'

I looked at the couple at the table next to ours, a man and a woman who had eaten their meal in a more or less unbroken silence. She had kept her handbag on the table in front of her plate, as though she was worried it might be stolen. It sat there between them and both of them glanced at it occasionally.

'But did you tell Konstantin that you had heard him?' Melete said. 'That morning, while you were waiting for the taxi, did you admit it?'

'Yes,' Elena said. 'He was embarrassed, of course, and said it had been a thoughtless comment, that it didn't mean anything, and in a way I believed him and it was a relief, but in my heart I thought – why bother to speak at all? Why say anything, if you can just take it back the next minute? Yet of course I wanted it to be taken back. And even thinking about it now the whole thing seems slightly unreal, as though by allowing it to be taken back I can no longer be sure that it actually happened. Anyway,' she continued, 'the taxi came and he got in it and left, both of us friends again, but afterwards I had the feeling of a stain, something small but permanent, like a little stain that ruins the whole dress – I imagined all the years passing, and us having children, and me never being able to forget the way he had shaken his head and said no when someone had asked him whether he wanted them. And him perhaps remembering that I was a person capable of invading his privacy and judging him on what I had found. This idea made me want to run away from him, from our apartment and the life we have together, to hide myself somewhere, in something unspoiled.'

There was a silence, into which the noise from the surrounding tables steadily flowed. We drank the soft, dark wine, so soft it could barely be felt on the tongue.

'Last night I had a dream,' Melete said presently, 'in which I and several other women, some of whom were friends of mine and some of whom were strangers, were trying to get into the opera. But all of us were bleeding, pouring out menstrual blood: it was a kind of pandemonium, there at the entrance to the opera house. There was blood on our dresses, dripping down into our shoes; every time one woman stopped bleeding another started, and the women were placing their bloodied towels in a neat pile by the door to the building, a pile that got bigger and bigger and that other people had to pass to get in. They looked at us as they passed, men in their dinner jackets and bow ties, in absolute disgust. The opera began; we could hear the music coming from inside, but we couldn't seem to get ourselves across the threshold. I felt a great anxiety', Melete said, 'that all of this was somehow my fault, because I was the one who had first noticed the blood, noticed it on my own clothes, and in my tremendous shame I seemed to have created this much bigger problem. And it strikes me', she said to Elena, 'that your story about Konstantin is really a story about disgust, the disgust that exists indelibly between men and women and that you are always trying to purge with what you call frankness. As soon as you cease to be frank, you see a stain, you are forced to acknowledge imperfection, and you want only to run away and hide in shame.'

Elena nodded her golden head, and put her hand across the table to touch Melete's fingers.

When she was a child, Melete continued, she used to suffer from the most terrible attacks of vomiting. It was a quite debilitating condition that persisted for several years. The attacks always occurred at exactly the same time of day and under exactly the same circumstances, the hour when she would return from school to the house she shared with her mother and stepfather. Understandably enough, her mother was very distressed by Melete's suffering, which had no apparent cause and therefore seemed to be nothing less than a criticism of her own way of life and the man she had introduced into the household, a man her only child refused – as though by a point of principle – to love or even to recognise. Every day at school, Melete would forget about the vomiting, but then as it became time to go home she would feel the first signs of its approach, a feeling of weightlessness, almost as though the ground were giving way under her feet. She would hurry back to the house in a state of anxiety, and there, usually in the kitchen, where her mother was waiting to give her her afternoon snack, an extraordinary nausea would start to grow. She would be taken to the sofa to lie down; a blanket would be put over her, the television switched on, and a bowl left by her side; and while Melete retched, her mother and stepfather would spend their evening together in the kitchen, talking and eating dinner. Her mother had taken her to doctors, therapists, and finally a child psychoanalyst, who suggested – much to the mystification of the adults who were paying his bill – that Melete take up a musical instrument. He asked her whether there was any instrument in particular she had ever thought of playing, and she said, the trumpet. And so, reluctantly, her mother and stepfather had bought her a trumpet. Now, every day after school, instead of the consuming prospect of the vomiting, she had before her the prospect of blowing through the brass instrument to produce its great rude noise. In this way she had made manifest her disgust in flawed humanity, and also managed to interrupt those tête-à-têtes over supper in the kitchen, which could never again be conducted in quite the same way, without her as their victim.

'Lately,' she said, 'I have taken the trumpet out of its case and started practising. I play it in my little apartment.' She laughed. 'It feels good to be making that rude noise again.'

On the way back down the hill, Elena said she would have to stop off in Kolonaki Square to get her motorbike. She offered Melete a lift on the back, since they lived close to one another. There was plenty of room for two people, she told me, and it was the quickest way. She had travelled all over Greece like that with her oldest female friend, Hermione, the two of them even taking the bike on the ferries out to the islands with just some money and their swimming costumes, finding beaches down dirt tracks where there wasn't another person to be seen. Hermione had clung to her down some formidable mountainsides, she said, and they had never yet fallen off. Looking back, those were some of the best times of her life, though at the time they had had the feeling of a prelude, a period of waiting, as though for the real drama of living to begin. Those times had more or less gone, now that she was with Konstantin: she wasn't sure why, because he would never have stopped her from going off travelling with Hermione, in fact he would have liked it, as modern men always liked it when you proved your independence from them. But it would have felt like a fake somehow, she said, a copy, to try to become those girls again, hurtling down those dirt roads, never knowing what they would find at the end of them.

# IX

The assignment was to write a story involving an animal, but not all of them had completed it. Christos had invited them to go Lindy Hop dancing the previous evening; it had been a late and exhausting night, though Christos himself appeared unaffected. He sat there beaming with his arms folded, proud and fresh, laughing startlingly and loudly at their observations concerning the evening's events. He had got up early to write his story, he said, though he had found it hard to introduce an animal into his chosen subject-matter, which was the hypocrisy of our religious leaders and the failure of public commentators to subject them to the proper scrutiny. How would ordinary people ever become politicised, if the intellectuals of our time didn't show them the way? This was something about which he and his close friend Maria, incidentally, disagreed. She was an adherent of the philosophy of persuasion: it sometimes did more harm than good, she said, to try to force people to recognise unpleasant truths. One had to stay close to the line of things, close but separate, like a swallow swooping over the lineaments of the landscape, describing but never landing.

So he had struggled, Christos said, to bring an animal into his account of the scandalous conduct of two orthodox bishops at a recent public debate. But then it had occurred to him that this was perhaps what I had intended. I had wanted, in other words, to present him with an obstruction that would prevent him from going the way he was naturally inclined to go, and would force him to choose another route. But try as he might he could not think of any way of getting an animal into the debating chamber of a public building, where it had no right to be. Also his mother kept disturbing him by coming in and out of the dining room, the room in their small apartment that was least often used and where, consequently, he usually did his studies, spreading his books and papers all over the old mahogany table that had stood there for as long as he could remember. Today, however, she had asked him to clear his things away. A number of family members were coming to dinner and she wanted to clean the room thoroughly in preparation for their arrival. He asked her, with some irritation, to leave him be – I'm trying to write, he said, how can I write without my books and papers and with you coming in all the time? He had completely forgotten about this dinner, which had been arranged a long time ago, and was being held in honour of his aunt and uncle and cousins from California, who had returned to Greece for their first visit in many years. His mother was not, he knew, looking forward to the occasion: this particular branch of the family was boastful and ostentatious, and his aunt and uncle were forever writing letters to their Greek relatives that pretended to be loving and concerned but were really just opportunities for them to brag about how much money they had in America, how big their car was, how they had just had a new swimming pool installed and how they were too busy to come home for a visit. And so, as he had said, many years had passed in which he and his mother had not laid eyes on these relatives, except in the photographs they regularly sent, which showed them standing in bright sunlight beside their house and car, or else at Disneyland or outside the Hard Rock Cafe, or in some other place where you could see the big Hollywood sign in the background. They also sent photographs of their children, graduating from this college or that, in mortar boards and furred gowns, baring their expensive teeth against a fake blue sky. His mother displayed these photographs dutifully on the sideboard; one day, he knew she hoped, Christos too would complete his degree and she would be able to put his photograph

203

beside them. The photograph Christos hated most of all was the one of his handsome, grinning, muscular cousin Nicky, which showed him in some sort of desert setting with a giant snake – a boa constrictor – draped across his shoulders. This image of superior manhood had often haunted him from the sideboard, and looking at it now, he no longer felt annoyed with his mother: he felt sympathy for her, and wished that he had been a better and braver son. So he stopped what he was doing and helped her clear things away.

Georgeou put his hand up. He had observed, he said, that where yesterday we had the windows open and the door shut, today it was the other way around: the windows were sealed, and the door to the corridor was significantly ajar. Also, he wondered whether I had noticed that the clock had moved. It was no longer on the wall to the left, but had taken up the mirroring position on the wall opposite. There was certainly an explanation for the movement of the clock, but it was hard to think of what it might be. If an explanation occurred to me perhaps I would inform him, because as things stood he found the situation disturbing.

He had finished writing his story, Christos continued, on the bus here, after he had realised that the photograph of Nicky had after all given him a way out of his dilemma. One of the bishops has a hallucination, there in the debating chamber: he sees a huge snake, draped over the shoulders of the other bishop, and realises that this snake symbolises the hypocrisy and lies they have both been spouting. He vows then and there to be a better man, to tell only the truth, and never to mislead and deceive his people again.

Christos folded his arms again and beamed around the room. Presently Clio, the pianist, put her hand up. She said that she too had found it difficult to write about an animal. She knew nothing about animals: she had never even had a pet. It would have been impossible, given the exacting nature of her practice schedule even in early childhood. She would have been unable to look after it and give it the attention it needed. But the assignment had caused her to notice things differently: walking home, she had not looked at the things she usually looked at but instead had become, as she walked, increasingly aware of birds, not just the sight of them but also their sound, which, once she attuned her ear to it, she realised she could hear constantly all around her. She remembered then a piece of music she had not listened to for a long time, by the French composer Olivier Messiaen, written during his internment in a prisoner-of-war camp during the Second World War. Some of it was based, or so she had understood, on the patterns of birdsong he had heard around him while under detention there. It struck her that the man was caged while the birds were free, and that what he had written down was the sound of their freedom.

It was interesting to consider, Georgeou said, that the role of the artist might merely be that of recording sequences, such as a computer could one day be programmed to do. Even the question of personal style could presumably be broken down as sequential, from a finite number of alternatives. He sometimes wondered whether a computer would be invented that was influenced by its own enormous knowledge. It would be very interesting, he said, to meet such a computer. But he sensed that any system of representation could be undone simply by the violation of its own rules. He himself, for instance, leaving the house this morning had noticed, perched on the verge beside the road, a small bird that could only have been described as being lost in thought. It was gazing at something in that unfocused way one observes in people trying, for example, to work out a mathematical problem in their heads, and Georgeou had walked right up to it while it remained completely oblivious. He could have reached out and grabbed it with his hand. Then, finally, it noticed he was there and nearly jumped out of its skin. He did have some concerns about that bird's capacity for survival, however. His own story, he added, was based entirely on his personal experience, and described in detail a conversation he had had with his aunt, who was researching mutations in certain particles at a scientific institute in Dubai. His only invention had been the addition of a lizard, which had not been there in reality, but which in the story his aunt kept tucked safely under her arm while they spoke. He had showed the story to his father, who had confirmed that all the details were accurate, and who said he had enjoyed witnessing the conversation, whose subject interested him, for a second time. He described the lizard, if Georgeou remembered the phrase correctly, as a nice touch.

Sylvia said she had written nothing at all. Her contribution yesterday, if I recalled, had in fact concerned an animal, the small white dog she had seen perched on the shoulder of the tall dark man. But after the others had spoken she wished she had chosen something more personal, something that would have allowed her to express an aspect of her own self, rather than a sight that was asking, as it were, to be seen. She had looked out for that man again on the train home, as it happened, feeling that she had something to say to him. She wanted to tell him to take the dog off his shoulder and let it walk, or better still get a dog that was ordinary and ugly, so that people like her wouldn't feel so distracted from their own lives. She resented him for his attention-seeking behaviour and for the fact that he had made her feel so uninteresting; and now here she was, mentioning him in class for the second time!

Sylvia had a small, pretty, anxious face, and great quantities of ash-coloured hair worn in maidenly rolls and tresses – which she touched and patted frequently – around her shoulders. In any case, she continued, she obviously didn't see him again on the way home, because life wasn't like that: she returned to her apartment, which since she lives alone was exactly as she had left it that morning. The telephone rang. It was her mother, who always phones her at that time. How was school today, her mother wanted to know. Sylvia works as a teacher of English literature, at a school in the suburbs of Athens. Her mother had forgotten she had the week off to do the writing course. 'I reminded her of what I had been doing,' Sylvia said. 'Of course, my mother is very sceptical about writing, so it's typical that she wouldn't remember. You should have gone on holiday instead, she said, you should have gone out to one of the islands with some friends. You should be living, she said, not spending more time thinking about books. To change the subject I said to her, Mum, tell me something you've noticed today. What would I have noticed?

she said. I've spent all day in the house, waiting for the man to come and fix the washing machine. He never even turned up, she said. After our conversation I went and looked at my computer. I had set my students an essay assignment, and the deadline had now passed, but when I checked my emails I saw that not a single one of them had sent the essay. It was an essay about *Sons and Lovers* by D. H. Lawrence, the book that has inspired me more than anything else in my life, and none of them had a single word to say about it.

'I went and stood in my kitchen,' she continued, 'and thought about trying to write a story. But all I could think of was a line describing the exact moment I was living in: *a woman stood in her kitchen and thought about trying to write a story*. The problem was that the line didn't connect to any other line. It hadn't come from anywhere and it wasn't going anywhere either, any more than I was going anywhere by just standing in my kitchen. So I went to the other room and took a book off the shelf, a book of short stories by D. H. Lawrence. D. H. Lawrence is my favourite writer,' she said. 'In fact, even though he's dead, in a way I think he is the person I love most in all the world. I would like to be a D. H. Lawrence character, living in one of his novels. The people I meet don't even seem to *have* characters. And life seems so rich, when I look at it through his eyes, yet my own life very often appears sterile, like a bad patch of earth, as if nothing will grow there however hard I try. The story I started to read', she said, 'was called "The Wintry Peacock". It is an autobiographical story,' she said, 'in which Lawrence is staying in a remote part of the English countryside in winter, and one day when he is out on a walk he hears an unusual sound and discovers that it is a peacock trapped out on the hillside, submerged in the snow. He returns the bird to its owner, a strange woman at a nearby farm who is waiting for her husband to return home from the war.

'At this point,' she said, 'I stopped reading: for the first time, I felt that Lawrence was going to fail to transport me out of my own life. Perhaps it was the snow, or the strangeness of the woman, or the peacock itself, but suddenly I felt that these events, and the world he described, had nothing to do with me, here in my modern flat in the heat of Athens. For some reason I couldn't bear it any longer, the feeling that I was the helpless passenger of his vision, so I closed the book,' she said, 'and I went to bed.'

Sylvia stopped speaking. My phone rang on the table in front of me. I saw the number of Lydia at the mortgage company flashing on the screen, and I told the group that we would take a short break. I went out and stood in the corridor among the notice-boards. My heart was beating uncomfortably in my chest.

'Is that Faye?' Lydia said.

Yes, I said.

She asked me how I was today. She could hear from my dial tone that I was abroad, she said. Where-abouts are you? Athens, I said. That sounds nice, she said. She was sorry she hadn't been in touch earlier. She'd been out of the office the last couple of days. A few of them in the department had been given some corporate seats for Wimbledon: yesterday she'd watched Nadal get knocked out, which was a big surprise. Anyway, she hoped it wasn't going to spoil my holiday, but she had to tell me that the underwriters had rejected my application to increase my loan. They don't need to give a reason, she said, when I asked her why. That was just their decision, based on the information they were provided with. As I say, she said, I hope it won't affect your holiday too much. When I thanked her for calling to tell me, she said it had been no problem at all. I'm sorry it couldn't have been with better news, she said.

I moved along the corridor and through the glass front doors at the entrance to the building and out into the ferocious heat of the street. I stood there in the glare while the cars and people passed, as though

I was expecting something to happen or for some alternative to present itself. A woman in a polka-dot sun hat with an enormous camera hung on a strap around her neck asked me the way to the Binyaki Museum. I told her and then I returned inside and went back to the classroom and sat down. Georgeou asked me if everything was all right. He had noticed, he said, that I had closed the door, and wondered if that meant I now wanted the windows to be opened. He was happy to perform that service if so. I told him to go ahead. He bounded out of his chair with such eagerness that he knocked it backwards. Surprisingly deftly, Penelope shot out her hand to catch it, and set it carefully back on its feet. She had been certain, she said somewhat enigmatically, that she would have nothing whatsoever to bring to class today, except her dreams, which were often so lurid and strange she thought she ought to tell someone about them. But generally speaking it was not possible, she had accepted after yesterday's class, for a person in her position to be a writer, someone whose time was not their own. And so she had spent the evening in the way she usually did, cooking dinner for her children and ministering to their ceaseless demands.

While they were eating the doorbell had rung: it was Stavros from next door, who had just dropped by to show them a puppy from the new litter his bitch had just produced. Of course the children were wild about this puppy: they left their food to get cold on its plates and went to stand around Stavros, begging in turn to be allowed to hold it. It was a very tiny puppy, its eyes barely open, and Stavros said they would have to be very careful, but he let each of them hold it one by one. 'I watched each child', she said, 'become transformed, as it received the puppy into its arms, into a creature of the utmost gentleness and caution, so that it was almost possible to believe the puppy had brought about an actual refinement in their characters. Each of them stroked the little soft head with their fingers and whispered into its ears, and this would apparently have gone on and on had Stavros not said that he needed to go. The puppies, he mentioned, were for sale; and at these words the children began to bounce up and down with the most genuine, infectious excitement, so that much to my own astonishment,' she said, 'I began to feel excited too. The thought of relenting, and of the love I would receive if I did, was almost irresistible. Yet my know-ledge of Stavros's bitch, who is a fat and disagreeable animal, was stronger. No, I said to him, we weren't going to have a dog; but I thanked him for showing it to us and he left. Afterwards the children were very disappointed. You always spoil everything, my son said to me. And it was only then, when the spell the puppy had cast had completely worn off, that logic returned to me, and with it a sense of reality that was so harsh and powerful it seemed to expose our household as mercilessly as if the roof had been torn off the building in which we stood.

'I sent the children to their rooms, without finishing their supper, and with my hands trembling I sat at the kitchen table and began to write. I had in fact once bought them a puppy, you see, two years before, under circumstances almost indistinguishable from those I have just recounted, and the fact that we had returned to that same moment, having learned nothing, made me see our life and particularly the children themselves in the coldest possible light. It was, as I say, two years ago now: the dog was a very pretty animal we called Mimi, with a curly tobacco-coloured coat and eyes like two chocolates, and when she first came to live with us she was so tiny and charming that the work I had to do looking after her was balanced against the pleasure the children took in playing with her and showing her off to their friends. It could almost be said that I didn't actually want them to have to clean up after Mimi, who made the most foul-smelling messes all over the house, for fear that their pleasure would be spoiled; but as Mimi grew bigger and more demanding I came to want them to take some responsibility for her, since it was through their choice – as I constantly told them – that we had got a dog in the first place. But very quickly they grew inured to these remarks: they didn't want to take Mimi for walks or clean up after her; what's more, they began to get annoyed by her barking, and by the fact that she would sometimes go into their rooms and create havoc and destroy their things. They didn't even want her in the sitting room with them in the evenings, because she wouldn't sit still on the sofa but paced around and around the room, obstructing their view of the television.

'Mimi, as well as quickly growing to be far bigger and more energetic than I had expected, was also obsessed with food, and if I took my eye off her for a moment she was up on the kitchen counters, foraging and eating everything she could find. I quickly learned to put things away, but I had to be very vigilant, and also to remember to shut all the doors in the house so that she couldn't go into the other rooms, doors the children were forever leaving open again; and of course I had to take her for walks, when she would pull me along so fast I thought my arm would come out of its socket. I could never let her off the lead, because her love for food sent her running off in all directions. Once she ran into the kitchen of a café by the park and was found by the furious chef eating a whole string of sausages he had left on the counter;

another time she snatched the sandwich right out of the hand of a man who was sitting on a bench eating his lunch. Eventually I realised I would have to keep her tied to me forever while we were out, and that in the house I was similarly bound to her, and it began to dawn on me that in getting Mimi for my children I had, without much thought, entirely given away my freedom.

'She was still a very pretty dog, and everybody noticed her. So long as I kept her on the lead, she would always receive the most lavish compliments from passers-by. Harassed as I was, I started to become curiously resentful and jealous of her beauty and of all the attention she got. I began, in short, to hate her, and one day, when she had been barking all afternoon and the children had refused to take her out, and I discovered her in the sitting room chewing to shreds a new cushion I had just bought while the children stared, unconcerned, at the television, I found myself seized by such an uncontrollable fury that I hit her. The children were deeply shocked and angry. They threw themselves on Mimi, to protect her from me; they looked at me as though I were a monster. But if I had become a monster, it was Mimi, I believed, who had made me one.

'For a while they reminded me constantly of the incident, but gradually they forgot about it, and so one day under similar provocations it happened again, and then again, until my hitting Mimi became something they almost accepted. The dog herself began to avoid me; she looked at me with different eyes and became very devious, sneaking around the house destroying things, while the children developed a very slight coolness in their manner towards me, a new sort of distance, which liberated me in a way but also made my life less rewarding. Perhaps to compensate for this feeling and to try to close the distance between us, I decided to make a great fuss of my son's birthday and stayed up half the night baking him a cake. It was a cake of the greatest beauty and extravagance, with chestnuts in the flour and shaved chocolate curls on top, and when it was finished I put it well out of Mimi's reach and went to bed.

'In the morning, after the children had gone to school, my sister stopped by to see me. In my sister's company I am always a little distracted from my own purpose; I have a sense that I need to perform things for her, to present them to her, to show her my life rather than let her see it naturally, as it really is. And so I showed her the cake, which she would have seen in any case as she was coming to the birthday party later. Just then there was the sound of a car alarm from the street, and thinking it must be her car – which was new, and which she disliked parking outside my house because the area, she says, is not as safe as where she lives – she panicked and ran outside. I followed her, because as I have already said, when I am with my sister I see things from her point of view rather than my own, am compelled to enter her vision, as I used to be compelled to enter her room when we were children, always believing it to be superior to my own. And as we stood out in the street making sure that her car was intact, which of course it was, I became aware of this feeling of having deserted my own life, as once I would desert my room; and I was suddenly filled with the most extraordinary sense of existence as a secret pain, an inner torment it was impossible to share with others, who asked you to attend to them while remaining oblivious to what was inside you, like the mermaid in the fairy story who walks on knives that no one else can see.

'I stood there while my sister talked, about her car and what might have set off the alarm, and felt this compelling pain of loneliness; in admitting which, I knew, I was also admitting the blackest vision of life. I knew, in other words, that something terrible would happen, was happening right then, and when we returned inside and found Mimi on the counter with her face thrust deep into the birthday cake, her jaws churning, I was not the slightest bit surprised.

She looked up as we came in, frozen in the act, the chocolate curls still hanging around her muzzle; and then she seemed to make a decision, for instead of jumping off the counter and running away to hide, she looked me defiantly in the eye and bending over it again, thrust her face wolfishly into the cake once more to finish it off.

'I crossed the kitchen and grabbed her by her collar. In front of my sister, I yanked her off the counter and sent her scrambling to the floor, and I proceeded to beat her while she yelped and struggled. The two of us fought, me panting and seeking to punch her as hard as I could, she writhing and yelping, until finally she succeeded in pulling her head free of the collar. She ran out of the kitchen, her claws scrabbling and sliding on the tiled floor, and into the hall, where the front door still stood open, and then out into the street, where she tore off up the pavement and disappeared.'

Penelope paused and placed her fingers first gently and then probingly to her temples.

'All afternoon,' she continued presently, 'the telephone rang. Mimi, as I have said, was a very distinctive and beautiful dog, and she was well known to people in the area, as well as to my acquaintances elsewhere in Athens. And so people were calling me to tell me they had seen her running away. She was seen everywhere, running in the park and the shopping centre, past the dry cleaner and the dentist's, past the hairdresser, past the bank, past the children's school: she ran everywhere I had ever been forced to take her, past the houses of friends and the piano teacher's house, the swimming pool and the library, the playground and the tennis courts, and everywhere she ran people looked up and saw her and picked up the telephone to tell me that they had seen her. Many of them had tried to catch her; some had given chase, and the window cleaner had driven after her for a while in his van, but no one had been able to catch her. Eventually she got to the train station, where my brother-in-law happened to be getting off a train: he phoned to say that he had seen her and tried to corner her, with the help of the other passengers and the station guards, and she had eluded their grasp. One of the guards had been slightly injured, colliding with a luggage trolley when he lunged to grab her tail; but in the end they had all watched her run off down the tracks, to where nobody knows.'

Penelope let out a great heaving breath and fell silent, her chest visibly moving up and down, her expression stricken. 'That is the story I wrote,' she said finally, 'at the kitchen table last night, after the visit of Stavros and the puppy.'

Theo said it sounded like the problem was that she had chosen the wrong dog in the first place. He himself had a pug, he said, and he had never experienced any difficulties.

At this, Marielle readied herself to speak. The effect was of a peacock bestirring its stiff feathers as it prepared to move the great fan of its tail. She had come dressed in cerise today, high-throated, with her yellow hair gathered up in a comb and a sort of mantilla of black lace around her shoulders.

'Once I too bought my son a dog,' she said in a shocked and quavering voice, 'when he was a little child. He loved it madly, and while it was still a puppy it was run down before his eyes by a car in the street. He picked up its body and carried it back into the apartment, crying more wildly than I have ever known a person to cry. His character was completely ruined by that experience,' she said. 'He is now a cold and calculating man, concerned only with what he can get out of life. I myself put my trust in cats,' she said, 'who at least can settle the question of their own survival, and while they might lack the capacity for power and influence, and might be said to subsist on jealousies and a degree of selfishness, also possess uncanny instincts and a marked excellence in matters of taste.

'My husband left me our cats,' she continued, 'in exchange for certain pre-Columbian artefacts he was extremely reluctant to lose sight of, but he claimed that a part of himself was left behind with them, to the extent that he almost feared being out in the world without the sense of guidance the cats provided. And it is true,' she continued, 'that his choices since then have been less blessed: he bought an etching by Klimt that afterwards was shown to be a fake, and has invested heavily in Dadaism, when anyone could have told him that public interest in that era was irreparably in decline. I, meanwhile, have been unable to avoid the most generous fondlings from the gods, even finding in the flea market a small bracelet in the form of a snake that I bought for fifty cents, and that my husband's friend Arturo caught sight of on my arm when we happened to meet one day on the street. He took it away to his institute to analyse it, and when he returned it, told me it had come from the tomb itself at Mycenae and was quite priceless, a piece of information I am certain he will have passed on to my husband in the course of their nightly conversations at the Brettos Bar.

'But cats, as I say, are jealous and discriminating creatures, and since my lover came to share my apartment they have been very slow to yield, despite his constant attentions to them, which as soon as his back is turned they instantly forget. He is unfortunately an untidy man, a philosopher, who leaves his books and papers everywhere, and while my apartment is not fragile in its beauty, it needs to be dressed a certain way to look its best. Everything is painted yellow, the colour of happiness and the sun but also, so my lover claims, the colour of madness, so that very often he needs to go out to the roof, where he stands and concentrates on the cerebral blue of the sky. While he is gone I feel the happiness returning; I start to put away his books, some of which are so heavy I can barely lift them with both hands. I have conceded, after a struggle, two shelves to him in my bookcase, and he kindly chose the ones at the bottom though I know he would have preferred the top. But the top shelves are high, and the works of Jürgen Habermas, of which my lover has a large collection, are as heavy as the stones they used to build the pyramids. Men went to their deaths, I tell my lover, in building these structures whose bases were so large and whose final point so small and distant; but Habermas is his field, he says, and at this stage of his life he will be offered no other to roam in. Is he a man or a pony? While he stands gazing on the roof this is the question I ask myself, almost nostalgic for my husband's appalling nature, which made me run so fast I always slept well at night. Sometimes,' she said, 'I retreat to my women friends, all of us weeping and weaving together, but then my lover will open the piano and play a tarantella, or bake a kid all afternoon in wine and cloves, and seduced by those sounds and smells I am back, lifting the rocks of Habermas and placing them on the shelves. But then one day I stopped, recognising that I couldn't hold it off any longer and that disorder had to reign; I painted the walls in eau de nil, took my own books off the shelves and left them lying there, allowed the roses to wither and die in their jars. He was delirious and said this had been an important step. We went out to celebrate, and returned to find the cats amok in the fallen library amidst a snowstorm of pages, their sharp teeth ravaging the spines even as we watched, with the Chablis still in our veins. My novels and leather-tooled volumes were untouched: only Habermas had been attacked, his photograph torn from every frontispiece, great claw-marks scorched across *The Structural Transformation of the Public Sphere*. And so,' she said in conclusion, 'my lover has learned to put his books away; and no longer does he bake or open the piano, and for this mixed blessing that is the shrinkage of his persona I have the cats – if not perhaps also my husband – to thank.'

Was it not the case, said Aris – the boy who the previous day had mentioned the putrefying dog – that we use animals as pure reflections of human consciousness, while at the same time their existence exerts a sort of moral force by which human beings feel objectified and therefore safely contained? Like slaves, he said, or servants, in whose absence their masters would feel vulnerable. They watch us living; they prove that we are real; through them, we access the story of ourselves. In our interactions with them we – not they – are shown to be what we are. Surely – for human beings – the most important thing about an animal, he said, is that it can't speak. His own story concerned a hamster he had when he was small. He used to watch it run in its cage. It had a wheel it ran around. It was always running – the wheel whirred and whirred. Yet it never went anywhere. He loved his hamster. He understood that if he loved it he had to set it free. The hamster ran away, and he never saw it again.

Georgeou informed me that the hour, according to the clock I could no longer see, because it was positioned directly behind my head, was now up. He had added on a few minutes for the time I had spent in the corridor: he hoped I was in agreement with that decision, which he had had to take alone, so as not to interrupt.

I thanked him for this information, and thanked the class for their stories, which, I said, had given me great pleasure. Rosa had produced a pink box

225

tied with a ribbon, which she passed to me across the table. These were almond cakes, she said, that she had baked herself, from a recipe her grandmother had given her. I could take them away with me; or, if I preferred, I could share them out. She had baked enough for each member of the class to have one, though since Cassandra hadn't turned up, there would be one left over. I untied the ribbon and opened the sweet-smelling box. Inside there were eleven little cakes, perfectly arranged in white frilled wrappers. I turned the box so that all of them could see what Rosa had done before passing them around. Georgeou said he was relieved to have been given the opportunity to examine the contents of the box, which he had noticed early on and had been somewhat anxious about, thinking there might be an animal inside.

# X

'Don't mind me,' said the woman who was sitting on Clelia's sofa when I came out of my bedroom at seven o'clock in the morning.

She was eating honey straight from the jar with a spoon. Two large suitcases stood on the floor beside her. She was an attenuated, whey-faced, corkscrew-haired person somewhere in her forties, with an unusually long neck and a rather small head, like that of a goose. Her voice had made quite a distinctive squawking sound, which added to the impression. I noticed the pale green colour of her small, unblinking, lashless eyes beneath severe black brows: she kept the lids slightly crinkled in a kind of grimace, as though for protection against the light. It was suffocatingly hot in the apartment. Her clothes – a wine-coloured velvet jacket, a shirt and trousers, and a pair of heavy-looking black leather boots – must have felt uncomfortable.

'I've just flown in from Manchester,' she explained. 'It was raining there.'

She was sorry to arrive so early, she added, but the

timing of her flight was such that short of going to sit in a café with her suitcases there was nothing else she could think of. The taxi driver had helped her carry them up the stairs, which was the least he could do, she said, after occupying the entire half-hour journey from the airport telling her in meticulous detail the plot of the science-fiction novel he was writing, she having made the mistake of telling him she had come to Athens to teach a writing course. His English was very good, though he spoke it with a strong Scottish accent: he had spent ten years driving a cab in Aberdeen, and had once given a ride to the writer Iain Banks, who had, so he said, been very encouraging. She'd tried to explain that she was a playwright, but then he'd said she was getting too technical. By the way I'm Anne, she said.

She stood up to shake my hand and then sat down again. I saw us as though through Clelia's big windows, two women shaking hands in an Athens apartment at seven o'clock in the morning. Her hand was very pale and bony, with a firm, anxious grip.

'This is a nice place,' she said, looking around. 'I didn't know what to expect – you never do know what to expect on these occasions, do you? I think I thought it would be more impersonal,' she said. 'I reminded myself on the way here to imagine the worst and it obviously did the trick.'

She'd anticipated, for some reason, she continued, being shoved in a box in some anonymous dusty block of flats, where dogs barked and children cried and people hung their washing on pieces of string tied to the window ledges, hundreds of feet above the ground; she'd even envisaged a motorway below, though perhaps it was just that she had seen such places from the cab on the way in, and had memorised them without really looking at them. But she supposed she had expected to be, in some way, mistreated. Quite why that was she wasn't sure. It was nice, she said, looking around again, to be pleasantly surprised.

She dug the spoon again into the honey jar and lifted it dripping to her mouth. 'Sorry about this,' she said. 'It's the sugar. Once I start I can't stop.'

I said there was food in the kitchen if she wanted it and she shook her head.

'I'd rather not know,' she said. 'I'm sure I'll get there soon enough. It's always different in a new place, but it's rarely better.'

I went to the kitchen myself, to make us some coffee. The room was hot and stuffy and I opened the window. The sound of distant traffic passed in from outside. The blank view of the white-painted backs of buildings was entirely in shadow. It was full of strange rectilinear shapes where new structures and extensions had been added, jutting out into the empty space between the two sides, so that in places they were nearly touching, like the two halves of something that had cracked all the way down the middle. The ground was so far below as to be out of sight, hidden in the shady depths of this narrow white ravine of blocks and rectangles where nothing grew or moved. The sun showed like a scimitar at the edge of the rooftops.

'That woman in the hall,' Anne said when I returned, 'gave me the fright of my life. When I first walked in, I thought she was you.' Her voice came out in a kind of squawk again and she put her hand to her long throat. 'I don't like illusions,' she added. 'I forget that they're there.'

She'd startled me several times too, I said.

'I'm a bit nervous generally,' Anne said. 'You can probably tell.'

She asked me how long I had been here, what the students were like and whether I had been to Athens before. She wasn't quite sure how the language barrier was going to work: it was a funny idea, writing in a language not your own. It almost makes you feel guilty, she said, the way people feel forced to use English, how much of themselves must get left behind in that transition, like people being told to leave their homes and take only a few essential items with them. Yet there was also a purity to that image that attracted her, filled as it was with possibilities for self-reinvention. To be freed from clutter, both mental and verbal, was in some ways an appealing prospect; until you remembered something you needed that you had had to leave behind. She, for instance, found herself unable to make jokes when she spoke in another language: in English she was by and large a humorous person, but in Spanish for instance – which at one time she had spoken quite well – she was not. So it was not, she imagined, a question of translation so much as one of adaptation. The personality was forced to adapt to its new linguistic circumstances, to create itself anew: it was an interesting thought. There was a poem, she said, by Beckett that he had written twice, once in French and once in English, as if to prove that his bilinguality made him two people and that the barrier of language was, ultimately, impassable.

I asked her whether she lived in Manchester, and she said no, she had just been up there to teach another course, and had had to fly straight from there to here. It was a bit exhausting but she needed the money. She had hardly done any writing lately – not that you got rich from writing plays, at least not the kind of plays she wrote. But something had happened to her writing. There had been – well, you'd call it an incident, and as a playwright she knew that the problem with incidents is that everything gets blamed on them: they become a premise towards which everything else is drawn, as though seeking an explanation of itself. It might be that this – problem would have occurred anyway. She didn't know.

I asked her what the problem was.

'I call it summing up,' she said with a cheerful squawk. Whenever she conceived of a new piece of work, before she had got very far she would find herself summing it up. Often it only took one word: *tension*, for instance, or *mother-in-law*, though strictly speaking that was three. As soon as something was summed up, it was to all intents and purposes dead, a sitting duck, and she could go no further with it. Why go to the trouble to write a great long play about jealousy when *jealousy* just about summed it up? And it wasn't only her own work – she found herself doing it to other people's, and had discovered that even the masters, the works she had always revered, allowed themselves by and large to be summed up. Even Beckett, her god, had been destroyed by *meaninglessness*. She would feel the word start to rise, and she would try to hold it down but it kept coming, rising and rising until it had popped irreversibly into her head. And not just books either, it was starting to happen with people – she was having a drink with a friend the other night and she looked across the table and thought, *friend*, with the result that she strongly suspected their friendship was over.

She scraped her spoon around the bottom of the honey jar. She was aware, she said, that this was also a cultural malaise, but it had invaded her inner world to the extent that she herself felt summed up, and was beginning to question the point of continuing to exist day in and day out when *Anne's life* just about covered it.

I asked her what the incident – if that was the word she had used – what the incident was that she had referred to earlier. She took the spoon out of her mouth.

'I was mugged,' she squawked. 'Six months ago. Someone tried to kill me.'

I said that was awful.

'That's what people always say,' she said.

She had by now finished the honey and was licking every last trace of it off the spoon. I asked whether I really couldn't get her something else to eat, since she was obviously so hungry.

'I'd better not,' she said. 'As I said, once I start I can't stop.'

I suggested it might help if I gave her something defined, something limited whose ending was clear.

'Maybe,' she said doubtfully. 'I don't know.'

I opened the pink box Rosa had given me, which was sitting on the coffee table between us, and offered her the single cake that remained. She took it and held it in her hand.

'Thank you,' she said.

One consequence of the incident, she said, was that she had lost the ability to eat in a normal way – whatever that was. She supposed she must have known how to do it once, because she had got this far without ever really thinking about eating, but she couldn't for the life of her remember how she had, or what she had eaten for all those years. She used to be married, she said, to a man who was a very good cook and who possessed generally an almost fanatical sense of order around food. The last time she had seen him, which was several months ago, he had suggested they go for lunch. He had chosen a fashionable restaurant, of a kind she no longer went to, for reasons of economy and also, she supposed, because she now lacked the necessary sense of en-titlement, in that she felt she had no right to be in such places any more. She had sat and watched him order and then slowly consume a starter, main course and dessert, each dish very moderate and in its own way perfect – the starter had been oysters and the dessert, if she recalled, had been fresh strawberries with a dash of cream – followed by a small espresso

234

which he had downed in one swallow. She herself had ordered a side salad. Afterwards, when they had parted, she had passed a donut shop and had gone inside and bought four donuts, which she consumed one after the other standing in the street.

'I've never told anyone that before,' she said, raising Rosa's cake to her lips and taking a bite.

Watching him eat the food, she continued, she had experienced two feelings that seemed directly to contradict one another. The first was longing; and the second was nausea. She both wanted and didn't want whatever it was that sight – the sight of him eating – had invoked. The longing was easy enough to understand: it was what the Greeks called *nostos*, a word we translated as 'homesickness', though she had never liked that word. It seemed very English to try to pass off an emotional state as a sort of stomach bug. But that day she had realised that *homesickness* just about summed it up.

Her ex-husband had not been much help after the incident. They were no longer married, so she supposed she had been wrong to expect it, but all the same it had surprised her. When it happened, he was the first person she thought to call – out of habit, it might seem, but if she were honest she still regarded them as being bound in some indissoluble sense. Yet it was immediately apparent, when she spoke to him on the phone that day, that he did not share her view. He was polite, distant and curt while she was angry, sobbing and hysterical: *polar opposites* was the phrase that had, during those difficult moments, popped into her mind.

It was through other people, some of them strangers, that the incident had to be unravelled: policemen, counsellors, one or two good friends. But it had been a descent into chaos, a whirling realm of non-meaning, in which the absence of her husband had felt like the absence of a magnetic centre so that without it nothing made any sense at all. The polarisation of man and woman was a structure, a form: she had only felt it once it was gone, and it almost seemed as though the collapse of that structure, that equipoise, was responsible for the extremity that followed it. Her abandonment by one man, in other words, led directly to her attack by another, until the two things – the presence of the incident and the absence of her husband – came almost to seem like one. She had imagined the end of a marriage, she said, to be a slow disentangling of its meanings, a long and painful reinterpretation, but in her case it hadn't been like that at all. At the time, he had got rid of her so efficiently and so suavely that she had felt almost reassured even as she was being left behind. He had perched beside her in his suit